D1562382

TWO TRAINS RUNNING

LUCIUS SHEPARD

GOLDEN GRYPHON PRESS • 2004

Copyright © 2004 by Lucius Shepard

Cover illustration copyright © 2004 by John Picacio

Edited by Marty Halpern

LIBRARY OF CONGRESS CATALOGUING-IN-PUBLICATION DATA
Shepard, Lucius.
   Two trains running / Lucius Shepard. – 1st ed.
     p.   cm.
   ISBN 1-930846-23-1 (alk. paper)
    1. Tramps—Fiction.   2. Tramps—West (U.S.)   3. Railroad travel—
Fiction.   4. Railroad travel—West (U.S.)   5. Homeless persons—Fiction.
6. Homeless persons—West (U.S.)   7. West (U.S.)—Social life and
customs.   8. West (U.S.)—Social life and customs—Fiction. I. Title.
   PS3569.H3939   T87   2004
   813'.54—dc22

                             2003018481

Printed in the United States of America.

First Edition

* * *

Contents

To Ben and Patrizia

* * *

Introduction: The Steel

SEVERAL YEARS AGO I CONTRACTED TO DO AN article for *Spin* magazine concerning a hobo organization called the FTRA (Freight Train Riders of America), a group that certain elements of law enforcement claimed was a hobo mafia responsible for—among other crimes—hundreds of murders, drug running on a massive scale, and the derailing of trains. As a result, I wound up hopping freights over the span of a couple months. I talked to train tramps in hobo jungles, urban squats, wino bars, at a supermax prison, and in various other venues. For a time I traveled with a hobo whom I called Madcat in the article, holding back his real name for fear he might suffer reprisals from those who did not like what I wrote about them. In Madcat's company I experienced a fair sampling of hobo life. It's a life that has little connection with the commonly held, somewhat folkloric view of hobos, one chiefly conveyed by stories and songs and images that reference the Depression era, portraying hobos—or as they prefer to be distinguished these days, train tramps—as colorful kings-of-the-road, lazy, easy-going, good-time-loving, stogie-smoking gents who might be prone to a little drunkenness, a little petty larceny, but nothing worse than that. Though this image may loosely fit the contemporary train tramp, it scarcely describes them. While some of the men and women I met on the rails were seriously dysfunctional, the remainder were more-or-less whole. They were not truly homeless, not impoverished due to fate—they had simply declined, for one reason or another, society's invitation to join and claimed to be fulfilled by their vagrant lives. They enjoyed being able to indulge laziness and substance abuse, and enjoyed, too, the brotherhood they found on the rails ("brotherhood" and "sisterhood" were words I often heard used to evoke the chief virtue of the lifestyle). Yet I would characterize few of them as easy-going. Surrounded by violence, generally in poor health, afflicted with psychological difficulties resulting from the stress of their day-to-day existence, they all passed a significant portion of their time in states of aggravation, fear, anxiety, and delirium. When I would press them as to the reason they continued to live as they did, the vast majority responded in kind: the trains.

There's no doubt that riding on a freight car as it carries you through some moonlit, mysterious corner of the American night is a rush like mystical whiskey for anyone with half an imagination. It's loud, uncomfortable, and a lot of the time it's damn cold, but it's also romantic. You're riding with ghosts, those of Jack Kerouac and Jack London and Ernest Hemingway, and all the ghosts of famous hobos that only hobos have ever heard of, and the fact that it's illegal and a little dangerous makes the moonlight extra silvery, and your bottled water tastes extra silvery, too. Working at my desk sometimes, I'll find myself transported back to a rattling, rushing moment and remember how it felt to be lost and alone in America, to be seeing the country from a perspective not many of us achieve. In my head I've got a file of snapshots of things and places few people will ever have a chance to see. A perfect little canyon in New Mexico, a trough of yellow stone brimful with golden late afternoon light, decorated with pines and grazing deer. Being almost stalled on an upgrade in the Rockies, sitting on the back of a grain car and watching a young woman, topless, wearing ragged shorts, her body adorned with tattoos of vines and leaves, emerge from the underbrush like a woodland spirit materializing and stare calmly at me from fifteen feet away (a sight whose magic was somewhat diminished when her boyfriend appeared, dragging their packs, and they hopped aboard the next car down). Standing in the Salt Lake City yard and seeing a pack of crusty punks—pierced, tattooed, grimy boys and girls—burst out from behind a string of rusting boxcars and scatter through the weeds, reminiscent in the suddenness of their passage, their deft speed and efficient flight, of wild animals started up by a threatening scent. It's one hell of an experience, but would I surrender my life to recapture it? Not hardly.

Most train tramps spend far more time in squats and jungles and missions than they do on the rails, but riding the trains is the core experience of hobo life and they venerate it because it's the only thing they have to venerate. All men, however debased their state, require a myth to sustain them. It may be a god, a devil, a lover, a dream of success or glory—whatever its nature, whether or not it reflects the least reality, we are moved to mythologize it, because our assumed intimacy with this presence elevates our self-esteem. For the hobo, whose functional relationship with the world is severely circumscribed, the train is the sole object worthy of deification. He conceives of it as embodying a romantic menace deserving of respect, this being the quality of which he feels most bereft. It is the trains, then, two-million-ton beasts with electric hearts and diesel blood, that function as god in the hobo pantheon, a god with whom he likes to believe he maintains a symbiotic relationship, one who transports him to places and experiences inaccessible to ordinary men, and whom he commonly refers to as the Steel.

I've talked to elderly train tramps, men in their sixties and seventies, who claim to have known Depression-era hobos, and from what I can gather, the freight trains have always been mythologized by those who rode them; but though it has never been other than difficult, it seems that hobo life was not so miserable or rife with danger in the old days as it can be now; thus I am convinced that the mythologizing of the trains has become more self-consciously devotional, an attitude necessary to sustain some men's commitment to the life. Certainly this is true with regards to a man named Big Sky Dave whom I encountered one night underneath a system of overpasses on the edge of Portland, Oregon, where the interstate merged a series of exchanges, a contemporary wasteland mapped by mattes of rotted cardboard and defiles filled with broken bottles and crushed cans. Everywhere were the signs of a fugitive existence. Lost shoes, message graffiti, discarded clothing. There were pillars all around, the lights of the city showing blurred through fog, like the lights of a distant coast, and I spotted Dave sitting in a meditative pose beside an abutment in a spot where the fog had thinned. He appeared to be in his forties. Gaunt and rawboned, with large callused hands. Black hair threaded with gray hung to his shoulders. Dwarfed by the sweep of dirty concrete above him, he radiated an air of detachment and had about him a dynamic placidity such as you might associate with a librarian or a funeral director, of someone constantly forced to speak in soft tones. He wore an old army jacket with HENDERSON, R. G. stenciled on the pocket. It may or may not have been his real name.

The expanse of concrete directly above Dave's head had been tagged with the brightly colored and skillfully rendered image of a demonic-looking locomotive, red lightnings spraying from its stack. A couple of cans of spray paint lay on the ground next to him, leading me to assume that he must be the artist. Naturally we mistrusted one another. Trust is a commodity not easy to come by in such circumstances. But after a while we fell to talking and Dave's conversation, though it skated over a variety of subjects—politics; freight schedules; which local beer had the highest alcohol content; etc.—mainly centered upon trains. As we drank (few discussions one has with hobos are free of significant substance abuse), he pulled out a stack of spiral ring notebooks—they must have constituted nearly half the weight of his pack—and proceeded to read from the literally hundreds of tributes to trains that they contained. The majority of the poems and prose fragments he read were overly sentimental, often mawkishly so, but they all made clear that he viewed the trains in a quasi-religious context. He called them not only "the Steel," but when speaking of a specific train, he would sometimes refer to it as "the Creature." Among his writings were a handful of gems, in particular a long, singsongy ode to the old streamliner passenger trains of the '40s and '50s (for purposes of meter and rhyme, Dave used the word "streamline" to refer to them), whose chorus evoked a mournful train whistle:

"Streamline . . .
All aboard for China and the Nile
Streamline . . .
Everything I ever thought I cried . . . "

I asked Dave if the spray-painted train was his doing and he told me he always left the same picture when he stayed in a place for a few days. Try as I might, I couldn't redirect the course of the conversation. He was too drunk, too obsessed with his subject, with his evangelical desire to persuade me of the majesty of trains. His words grew almost unintelligible. Eventually he passed out. When I woke in the morning he was gone. After packing my belongings, I had a last look at the spray-painted locomotive, took a photograph of it, and as I glanced about at the ranks of great pillars, the high concrete arches, the slants of sunlight piercing down from the upper reaches of the interchange, for the first time I recognized how like churches were these all-but-deserted places on the edges of our cities. Like unfinished cathedrals whose congregations have run out of funds and moved on to try their luck elsewhere.

In contemplating this mini-collection, deciding to put together a magazine article with stories derived from the same material, I hoped the process by which the *real* is transformed into the *fictive* might be thereby illustrated, at least as regards my own work, and that this relationship might be interesting to certain readers. But in writing this introduction I've come to realize that perhaps the most significant function of the book is that it adds a small but hopefully interesting drop to the literature concerning hobos, a sketchy tradition that dates back to the end of the Civil War, when the first hobos, the defeated soldiers of the Confederacy, having no money, no horses, rode the rails en masse in order to return to their homes: You see them in old photographs, like flocks of gray crows inhabiting boxcar after boxcar, all staring listlessly, bleakly out at the world, drunk on blood and dying, an expression whose cousin one can still see today in the faces of train tramps drunk on less potent mixtures. It's a tradition that's unlikely to have many more additions. With increasingly effective high-tech security being utilized by the railroad companies, the freight yards are becoming harder and harder to infiltrate, and without access to slow-moving trains, train tramps may become—for all intents and purposes—extinct. According to the viewpoint of law enforcement and of society in general, this will be a good thing. For my part, even though most of the people in America have no awareness of hobos, I think we'll miss them—I think not having that color running through the veins of the culture will thin our national blood. When I consider my brief time on the rails, I recall initially not scenes of degradation or violence, but the solitudes in which I found myself. Freight routes cover portions of the country never seen by anyone apart from those who ride the trains, and there are places of great beauty that will be forgotten. With no one to look at them, even if only through drunken and corrupted eyes, it will be as if parts of our map have vanished, in a very real sense restoring that map to something resembling the unfinished depiction of the continent that was deemed accurate more than a century ago. I remember, too, the stories I was told. Men grown old before their time, with gray beards, rheumy eyes, and poisoned livers, gazing back along the violent, dissolute corridors of their lives and relating observations and experiences informed by an oddly genteel aesthetic: moments of kindness, of unexpected good fortune, of happy days and boxcar parties that lasted from California to the Dakotas. All that lovely illusion and truth about the freedom of the rails and the inebriated Zen-monk illuminations that attend it . . . all that will be gone if the freight companies have their way and rid the yards of the derelicts, the dented souls, the human rats who ride the Steel. As will the skinny, million-mile-long city of the rails with its vagrant populace and anarchic laws. It's a tough place to live, but there are many cities in America that offer fewer cultural rewards.

Perhaps I'm being too pessimistic here. Perhaps sufficient technology will filter down into the hobo jungles and in the near future, cybernetically savvy train tramps will confound heat and motion detectors, slip unseen into the yards and barnacle themselves to robot-driven bullet freights, becoming devotees and celebrants of the New Steel. Probably not. The dissolute nature of hobo life, its fundamental lack of competency, would seem to lobby against this possibility. At the least it's an idea for another story and maybe in the end that's what is important. The world is made of stories. A man's life is a cloud of entangled narratives, and history a wagging tongue. And so as long as there are stories to be told about hobos, they'll continue in the way we all continue, products of our own myths, heroes in a misperceived and diminutive cause.

Two Trains Running

The FTRA Story

THE MAN WHO CALLS HIMSELF MISSOULA MIKE has passed out again, slumped onto his side, clutching a nearly empty quart bottle of vodka. His face is haggard, masked by grime and a prophet's beard gone to gray; his clothes are filthy. He appears to be in his sixties, but just as likely he's an ill-used forty-five. He coughs, and a wad of phlegm eels from his mouth, nests in the beard. Then, waking, he props himself on an elbow and stares wildly out at me from his lean-to. The glow from our dying camp-fire deepens his wrinkles with shadow, flares in his eyes, exposes stained teeth, and, ghoulishly underlit, his features resemble those of a Halloween mask, a red-eyed hobo from hell.

"Punk-ass camp thieves!" he says, veering off in a conversational direction that bears no relation to what we've been discussing. "They don't come 'round fuckin' with me no more."

Six inches of vodka ago, when Mike was capable of rational speech, he promised to reveal the secrets of the FTRA (Freight Train Riders of America), a shadowy gang of rail-riding transients characterized by elements of the press as the hobo mob. In return, he extracted my promise not to use his real name—if I did, he said, he would be subject to reprisals from his gang brothers. But no secrets have been forthcoming. Instead, he has engaged in a lengthy bout of chest beating, threatening other FTRA members who have

wronged him and his friends. Now he's moved on to camp thieves.
"They know Ol' Double M's got something for 'em." He grabs
the ax handle he keeps by his side, and takes a feeble swipe at the
air to emphasize his displeasure. "Cocksuckers!"

It occurs to me that I've talked to a lot of drunks recently, both
FTRA members and those who pretend to be FTRA. Articles and
TV pieces about the gang have generated a degree of heat on the
rails, causing security to tighten in and around the switchyards, and,
to avoid police attention, many FTRA members have put aside their
colors: bandanas ritually urinated upon by the participants in their
individual initiations. However, a number of unaffiliated hobos,
seeking a dubious celebrity, have taken to wearing them. Mike has
earned a degree of credence with me by keeping his colors in his
pack.

We're in a hobo jungle outside the enormous Union Pacific
switchyard at Roseville, California, a place where hobos camp for a
day or two until they can hop a freight—a longer stay may attract
the interest of the railroad bulls. The darkness is picked out by fires
tended by silhouetted figures. Shouts and laughter punctuate the
sizzling of crickets, and every so often the moan of a freight train
achieves a ghostly dominance. By day, the jungle had the appearance of a seedy campground, lean-tos and sleeping bag nests
scattered in among dry-leaved shrubs; but now, colored by my
paranoia, it looks like the bottom of the world, a smoky, reeking,
Dantean place inhabited by people who have allowed addiction or
financial failure or war-related trauma to turn them away from society, men and women whose identities have become blurred by years
of telling tall tales, by lying and showing false IDs, in the process
creating a new legend for themselves out of the mean fabric of their
existence.

A gangly hobo, much younger than Mike, comes over to bum a
cigarette. He peers at Mike and says, "Hey, man! You fucked up?"

Mike sits up, unsteady, managing to maintain a sort of tilted
half-lotus, but he says nothing.

"You the guy's been askin' 'bout the FTRA?" The gangly hobo
asks this of me and stoops to light his cigarette from an ember.

"Yeah," I say. "You FTRA?"

"Hell, no! Couple those motherfuckers lookin' to kill my ass."

"Oh, yeah? FTRA guys? What happened?"

The gangly hobo eyes me with suspicion. "Nothin' happened.
Just these pitiful fuckers decided they's goin' to kill me for somethin'
they thought I done. They been goin' round three months sayin' I

better keep the hell off the rails. But—" he spreads his arms, offering a target "—here I am. You know? Here I fuckin' am."

I try to question him further, but he's stalks off back to his camp. Mike's eyes are half-closed, his head begins to droop. Then a long plaintive blast of train sadness issues from the switchyard, and he stiffens, his eyes snap open. I get the idea he's listening to a signal from the back of beyond, a sound only he can interpret. His features are gathered in harsh, attentive lines, and with his ax handle held scepter-style, his beard decorated with bits of vegetation, in the instant before he loses consciousness, he looks dressed in a kind of pagan dignity, the image of a mad, primitive king.

The immense neighborhood of the rails, 170,000 miles of track, supports a population no larger than that of a small town; yet this population is widely variegated. Yuppie riders, prosperous souls for whom freight-hopping is a hobby. Eco-activist riders, most of them young, who view riding as a means of using the system against itself. Crusty punks, drunk punks, gutter punks: the order and suborders of the next generation of hobos. Pierced; tattooed; homeless; they travel from squat to squat on the trains. Then there are the hardcore hobos, those who spend their lives moving along the rails. Included in their number are the FTRA, who distinguish between their membership and the general run of hobos by calling themselves "tramps" (or "train tramps") and "trampettes."

This attenuated neighborhood and its citizenry constitute a grapevine that stretches coast to coast, conveying information such as how to get the best dumpster pizza in Denver, and where to find water near the Rio Grande yard in Pueblo. It also serves to carry horrific tales concerning the FTRA: a woman raped under a railroad bridge; a man left tied up and sodomized in a freight car, lying in his own blood and feces; two gutter punks and their dogs slaughtered by the gang in a boxcar, their girlfriends raped and then thrown from the train. Such stories are seconded by the majority of media reports. A week-long series on Portland's KOIN-TV identifies the FTRA as Freight Train Killers, and features an interview with a yuppie rider named K-Line who says she flung herself from a moving train to avoid rape by a group of gang members. A *Los Angeles Times* article speaks of a "mysterious brotherhood" and states that the gang has "set up rail lines out of Texas as drug-running corridors." The Spokane *Spokesman-Review*, under the heading "Killers Ride The Rails," says that "a racist gang of hobos may be responsible for 300 transient murders. . . ." Internet websites show pictures of hideously damaged corpses and print stories about FTRA atrocities. These and other print and electronic sources, inspired to a great extent by the exploits of hobo serial killer and alleged FTRA member Robert Silveria, paint a picture of a murderous criminal organization that holds barbarous initiation ceremonies involving rape and beating, along with ritual urination. Hardcore felons armed with weighted ax handles called Goon Sticks, who prey upon other transients, create an atmosphere of terror in switchyards and hobo jungles across the nation.

Estimates regarding the size of the FTRA's membership range from seven or eight hundred to upwards of two thousand—most riders would subscribe to the lower figure. Several police officers have put forward the idea that on occasion FTRA members serve as mules for biker gangs, bringing in heroin from Mexico; but none have gone so far as to say that this is endemic. The crimes with which FTRA hobos are most frequently charged are trespassing, disorderly conduct, and petty thievery, and these incidents are handled by railroad bulls, who usually let the offenders off with a ticket. Local cops don't spend much time in the rail yards, and, according to one detective, the average hobo's hygiene is so bad that most officers don't want them in their patrol cars.

There's little consensus on any subject among FTRA members themselves, not even concerning the origin of the group. The most believable story has it that a group of 12 hobos, Vietnam vets all, were partying beneath a bridge in Whitefish, Montana (or a bar in Libby, if you're to credit a variant version) in 1985, watching a freight train roll past. When an X-TRA container came into view, a hobo named Daniel Boone said jokingly, "We oughta call ourselves the FTRA—Fuck The Reagan Administration." Thus Daniel Boone is acknowledged to be the founder of the gang, an honor he reportedly now considers an embarrassment (he's given up life on the rails and become an itinerant preacher in the Bitterroot Mountains of Montana, living out of a camper van). But Mississippi Bones (a k a Marvin Moore, a gang member currently serving a sentence for first degree murder) claims the organization was founded in the 1940s by a black hobo named Coal Train, who died some thirty years later in a lean-to next to an abandoned Texaco station in Desert Center, California. Bones says he "carried the old man some wine" and sat with him a while, and has no doubt that he was the actual founding father.

The chief source for almost every news story concerning the FTRA is Officer Robert Grandinetti, a heavyset, affable man closing in on retirement age, who works out of the Office of Special Police

Problems in Spokane, Washington. He has made the gang his special project, not only pursuing and arresting them, but also devoting considerable time to raising the national consciousness as regards their particular menace. He's appeared on *America's Most Wanted* and makes presentations on the subject to federal commissions and law enforcement groups. Days, he patrols beneath the city's railroad bridges, areas where riders gather to "catch out" (the hobo term for hopping a freight). He carries a Polaroid camera with which he takes the picture of anyone he suspects of associating with or belonging to the FTRA, and these pictures are then mounted in hefty scrapbooks, along with mug shots and photographs of FTRA graffiti. He's compiled an extensive database on the gang's membership, and has a collection of FTRA artifacts, the most impressive being a Goon Stick (he calls it a Goonie Stick), an ax handle to one end of which has been welded a softball-sized lump of lead. He speaks with relish about the subject, expressing what seems a gruff fondness for certain gang members.

As we sit in his office, a fluorescent-lit cube with several desks and a prominently displayed employee award, Grandinetti utilizes visual aids—photographs, FTRA bandanas, and so forth—with the facile air of someone who has given the same show many times before (this due in part, I assume, to the fact that over the years he has lectured on police matters in the Spokane school system). His awareness of the FTRA derives from a series of unsolved murders in the early '90s, bodies found near the tracks along the Highline route from Cheney, Washington, to Sandpoint, Idaho, all with their jackets and shirts pulled over their heads, and their trousers pulled down. "If there'd just been a couple, I could buy them as accidents," he says. "But after six of them, the accident theory didn't fly." He goes on to say that there were over 450 trespass deaths on railroad property during the past year, and he believes a significant percentage of these were homicides perpetrated by the FTRA. To support this assumption, he cites cases in which the victim was struck by a train in a switchyard, yet there was little blood at the scene, suggesting that the victim was killed elsewhere, and the body placed on the tracks so the impact of the train would cover up the actual cause of death: blunt force trauma. But Grandinetti admits that in most of these cases it's impossible to determine whether the crimes were committed by the FTRA or independent hobos . . . or by anyone else, for that matter. Switchyards are generally situated in or near dangerous neighborhoods, and the idea that an indigent may have murdered a hobo is hardly unthinkable.

Over the course of an hour, Grandinetti sketches his vision of the gang. He talks about the various subgroups within the gang—the Goon Squad, the Wrecking Crew, STP (Start The Party). He explains "double-clutching"—the practice of obtaining emergency food stamps in one town, hopping a freight to the next, obtaining more food stamps there, and continuing the process until a hobo accumulated six or seven hundred dollars worth, which are then sold to a grocery store for 50 cents on the dollar. He describes how FTRA tramps will "hustle junk" (pick up scrap metal) and steal wire from freight yards, strip the copper and sell it in bulk to recycling businesses. Otherwise, he says, they "work the sign" (*Will Work For Food*) in order to get cash for their drugs and alcohol. He talks about the "home guard," homeless people who serve as procurers of drugs for gang members. But most of these practices are engaged in by hobos of every stripe, not just the FTRA, and little of what he says would be denied by the FTRA; though several members told me they would never steal from the railroads—you don't shit where you live.

To accept that the FTRA is a menace of the proportions Grandinetti claims—an organization that runs safe houses and has locked down switchyards all over the country—it seems necessary to believe further that there is some order to the gang's apparent disorder: Officers charged with obtaining revenue and determining goals. Chapters that communicate one with the other. Some sort of structure. Grandinetti tells me that from gang snitches he's learned of a group within the FTRA called "the Death Squad," whose function is to carry out hits. He claims that this group is led by their self-exiled founder, Daniel Boone. It's at this juncture that Grandinetti begins to preface his statements with the phrase "I can't prove it but . . ." and he says his informants have told him that two gang members were hired by right-wingers to derail an Amtrak train in Arizona a few years back. He's also heard a rumor that a white power group is attempting to organize the FTRA into a hobo army.

Under pewter skies, we drive out into the industrial wastes of the Spokane Valley and stop by the railroad tracks beneath the Freya Street bridge, its cement pillars and abutments spangled with FTRA graffiti—cartoon train tracks, swastikas, lightning bolts, along with messages and dates and train names. Among them is a section of wall devoted to a memorial for Horizontal John, an FTRA member who died of liver failure underneath the bridge the previous summer. Two hobos are camped here today, warming themselves by a small fire. Sheets of cardboard lie on the packed dirt nearby, and there are signs of past encampments: a worn-out shoe; a wadded pink cloth that might be a piece of blanket; empty cans; soggy news-papers. Neither of the two men are FTRA, but Grandinetti takes their pictures and checks them for warrants. One has a minor charge outstanding against him. Grandinetti's associate applies handcuffs and calls for a patrol car to take him to jail. Once this has been handled, Grandinetti strolls about, commenting on the graffiti. He's amused by one that warns AVOID JABBERJAW. Jabberjaw is a transient hooker rumored to have contracted AIDS, and Grandinetti says that this might be the ultimate cure for the FTRA.

I come across a series of messages left by a rider named Big Ed that insult and taunt the gang, and I make the comment that Big Ed must be pretty damn big to risk FTRA retribution. Grandinetti doesn't appear to have heard me, and I'm starting to think there's a lot more relating to the gang he's not hearing, that he's disposed to hear only what paints them in the most baleful light. I recall during our initial phone conversation, I mentioned that someone had told me he thought the FTRA was no more than an urban legend. Grandinetti became angry and said he didn't want to talk to anyone who held that view. It's important to him, I realize, that the FTRA poses a menace worthy of national attention, more of a menace than it perhaps is. I doubt he's trying to sell me anything—not consciously, anyway. He's a true believer, an evangel of the cause, and this work will comprise his legacy, his mark. I ask if he's going to miss all this when he retires, or if he's looking forward to going fishing. He looks offended, and tells me he's going to be kept very busy, thank you, traveling and lecturing about the FTRA.

After Grandinetti drives away, I wander about for a few minutes. These open spaces, under modern bridges enclosed by sweeping arches and pillars, have something of the feel of a church, as if they're cathedrals upon which construction was suddenly halted, now standing unused except by those who deface them, who have adapted to some less grandiose form of worship. This one, with its memorial wall and solitary pilgrim, the remaining hobo sitting head down and silent by his guttering fire, a slight bearded man in a shabby brown coat . . . it has that atmosphere more than most. The hobo turns his head to me, and it seems he's about to speak. But maybe there's too much authority in the air, too much of a police vibe. Without a word, he picks up the cloth sack containing his possessions and hurries off along the tracks.

The maximum security unit of the U.S. Penitentiary at Florence, Colorado, a red brick-and-glass chunk of modern penology that sits atop a subterranean high-tech Kafkaville of sanitized tile and electronic gates . . . it seems way too much prison for Mississippi Bones. He's a diminutive, frail-looking man of late middle age with a lined face, dressed in chinos and walking this day with a cane due to an injured foot. I meet him in a midsize auditorium ranged by rows of black vinyl-covered chairs, all bolted to the floor, where visitors and inmates can mingle under the watchful eyes of guards. This morning, except for a guard and a prison official who converse at a distance beside a desk, we're the only two people in the room. Every surface glistens. Dust is not permitted. I imagine there are secret angles involved in the room's design that will convey our slightest whisper to the area of the desk. Bones sits on the edge of his chair, hands on the head of his cane, and nods at the two men watching us. "I hate those sons of bitches," he says. "They're trying to listen to us, so we got to keep it down."

Bones is serving a 25-year-stretch for killing a fellow FTRA member named F-Trooper, a crime for which he does not apologize; he claims that if he hadn't done the deed, F-Trooper would have killed him—he had already tried it once, going after Bones when he was camped by the Rattlesnake Creek in Missoula, Montana, attacking him with a skinning knife, twisting it in his side until he had more-or-less removed three of Bones's ribs. The attack was provoked, Bones says, by F-Trooper's lust for his wife Jane.

It took Bones nearly a year to recover from his injuries. He underwent five operations, was stricken by a lung infection, and his weight dropped below 100 pounds. He was living on Percodans, and he expected to die. When he got back on his feet and went out again onto the rails, he ran into F-Trooper in the railyard in Missoula. F-Trooper, Bones says, had been planning on going to Helena to get his food stamps, but he changed his plans and decided to ride to Portland with Bones and his wife. Bones realized then that he was in danger from the man, and he says that he acted in self-defense.

At this juncture, Bones gets to his feet and demonstrates how he shot F-Trooper. He makes his right fist into a gun, places his forefinger against the top of my head, and pretends to fire down through my skull. It's an interesting moment. He no longer seems quite so frail.

"If I hadn't been drunk," Bones continues, "I'd a'never been charged. See, the boxcar we was in had a big red X marked on the side. That means they was goin' to break the car off and send it to the repair yard. But I was so drunk I didn't notice the mark. I figured F-Trooper would just go on off to Portland with the rest of the train."

Bones's relationship with the FTRA points up something that I'm coming to believe: that petty squabbles proliferate throughout the membership, and that ultimately the gang is more a danger to itself than to anyone else. During the interview, Bones voices bitterness toward a number of his FTRA brothers whom he says took money from the police to testify against him; he expresses particular loathing for a hobo named Moose who, he claims, had no knowledge of the crime and lied about it to the authorities. "I kept to the code," he says. "I didn't give up nothin' on nobody. And that's a lot more than some of those sons of bitches did for me."

Bones speaks of his affection for various gang members, but his attitude toward the rituals of the FTRA is less respectful. For one thing, nobody jumped him into the gang, he participated in no initiation; he started wearing the bandana and silver concho on his own authority. "I wore the red out of Arizona," he says, referring to the color of the bandanas worn by gang members who ride the old Southern Pacific routes. "Nobody would gainsay me." He scoffs at the notion that there is any sort of hierarchy in the gang. "You get six or seven together," he tells me, "and somebody'll call the shots. But that's all." He disputes the idea that rape and beating are part and parcel of FTRA initiations. "Once in a while some punk'll want to get in, and then there'll be a fight, but it ain't a regular thing. I never heard 'bout nobody getting raped." He's equally dismissive of the idea that the gang poses a serious menace.

"They're saying we're a threat to society, but the truth is, society is more a threat to us. Tramps get murdered all the time." He tells me about the time he was sleeping with his wife in a lean-to in the hobo jungle near Pasco, Washington, when a local opened fire on them from the bushes with a rifle.

"The thing you got to understand," he says, "hobos don't want much. FTRA or independent, it don't matter. They want a piece of dirt in the shade, they want their food stamps, they want something to drink, something to smoke, and something to screw."

Bones is scarcely what the law would consider a credible witness, certainly not so credible as Officer Grandinetti. He has an extensive arrest record, and he goes on at some length about "utilizing personal magnetism to subdue ruthless people," which speaks both to a measure of craftiness and a healthy streak of arrogance. He lies effortlessly; he's lied to me and subsequently admitted it. Like anyone in prison, he's working every angle he can, and I suspect he's working some angle with me. Not that I can fault him for it— he's alone, he has no idea where his wife is, no one writes him, and, except for his lawyer, I'm the only person from outside the walls with whom he's had contact. But despite this, and while I'm hesitant to make an informed judgment about his character based on a single interview, I find what he tells me, if not credible, then at least genuine in its essence. My acceptance of what he says probably has something to do with his enthusiasm for hoboing, for trains, for animals—especially his German shepherd, Star—and the outdoors. This enthusiasm seems an irreducible distillate of the man, and the longer we talk, the more what he says seems funded by that portion of his sensibility; and the more frequently he goes back to what we've previously discussed in order to, clarify some point, or to reshape a story so it better reflects the truth. It's as if he's gone past his natural suspicion of me, and is having a good time talking to someone from the world.

Our conversation turns to the trains, and when I tell Bones about my infant experiences on the rails, he lifts an eyebrow and says, "You've ridden?"

"Yeah, a little."

Bones continues looking at me for a long moment, his expression neutral, and I think he's trying to fit the information into his understanding of me, reassessing my potential. Or could be he's merely surprised. Then he grins, and I can see the face of the boy emerge from all those lines and wrinkles. It's a look of unalloyed pleasure, as if everything around us, walls and razor wire and guards, had vanished, and we were sitting on a patch of dirt somewhere warm, passing a bottle.

"Man, ain't it fun!" he says.

I'm riding in a boxcar south along the Columbia River, which must be nearly a mile wide at this point, and it's hard to tell which is the reflecting medium and which the source of light—the river, every eddy bearing a captive glint, or the starry sky above. The towering hills that follow the watercourse show dark and nearly featureless, all but their lowermost reaches in shadow, making it appear that the curtain of night has been gathered into great black folds at the edge of the bright stage it delimits. Though it's incredibly loud in the car, too loud for speech, something about the solitude and immensity of the scene, and perhaps the sense I have of the peculiarly American tradition of which I'm now a small part, the rail riders of the Civil War era, the hobos of the Depression, the FTRA . . . all this serves to describe a silence inside me, to shut me off from the rattling and the cold iron smells of the train, even from the noise of ambient thought, and after a while, emerging from an almost meditative state, I wonder if this is what Adman means by "the Drift."

Adman is the train name of Todd Waters, a brisk, fiftyish man with a neat gray beard who runs a successful Minneapolis advertising agency. He's been riding for more than twenty years, and admits to being what is called a "yuppie rider" or a "yuppie hobo." Most tramps use shoestrings to tie off their trouser cuffs when they're boarding a freight to prevent the fabric from catching on something and causing them to fall. Adman uses Velcro fasteners. When I met him he was wearing a sporty cap, and a denim jacket and trousers that appeared to be matching, and I thought he would look more natural steering a yacht than hopping a freight. He's given to comparing the quintessential hobo to a Hesse character whose purpose in life was "to make men homesick for their freedom," and he asserts that the experience of riding elevates him into a state he calls "the Drift," wherein it seems that his dreams and thoughts are colored not by his own past, but by the stars he's passing beneath and the places he's passing through.

I can't quite go there with Adman—I haven't yet found anyone on the rails who's made me homesick for my freedom. But you have to respect Adman because he's done something with his romantic zeal. Back in 1983 he created the Penny Route, encouraging people to contribute a penny for every mile he rode; he wound up raising more than a hundred thousand dollars for the National Coalition for the Homeless. Since then he's established himself as a respected figure in the hobo community, someone who can speak both to and for the transient rail population. What's troublesome about yuppie hobos in general, however, are the increasing numbers of sport riders and scenery freaks who sally forth onto the rails without regard for the risks involved. Should someone with a little fame—a minor rock star or a peripheral Kennedy relative—decide to hop a freight in order to research a part or just to feel that "Jack Kerouac thing," and then fall under the wheels of a boxcar, Officer Grandinetti will be turning up on every television program from *Nightline* to *American Journal*, wagging his finger and putting the bogeyman face of the FTRA on the tragedy, whether it applies or not, and the media frenzy will begin.

From the standpoint of the railroad companies, one might think that an intensified law enforcement focus on the subject of the FTRA, wrong-headed or not, would be a good thing, since it would probably result in even more security and fewer criminal incidents involving transients. But Ed Trandahl, a spokesman for Union

Pacific, laughed when I mentioned Grandinetti, and said, "Oh, yeah. We know about him." He went on to say that "The FTRA is a totally overblown deal. Union Pacific has thoroughly explored this with our railroad police, and there's no massive organization at work here. Our investigators have gone over hundreds of cases and we can't find any correlation to what Mr. Grandinetti is saying."

The 39-year-old hobo who brought the heat down onto the rails, Robert Joseph Silveria (a k a Sidetrack) has the word "Freedom" tattooed on his neck. In his case freedom is, indeed, just another word for nothing left to lose—on January 31,1998, he pled guilty to two counts of first degree murder, and was sentenced to two consecutive life sentences for having caused the deaths of Michael Clites, 24, and William Petit, Jr., 39, both transients, by means of blunt force trauma. He is due to be tried in Kansas and Florida on similar charges, and there is solid evidence connecting him with the murders of transients in Emeryville, Oregon, in West Sacramento, in Salt Lake City, and Whitefish, Montana. When I first interviewed Detective Mike Quakenbush of Salem, Oregon, who arrested Silveria, he told me that he believed Silveria was "good for a lot more murders than those with which he'd been linked," and, according to the San Francisco *Examiner*, Silveria himself told an uncle by marriage that he had killed 47 people out of a deep anger. In letters to a former jail acquaintance, Silveria declared that he was the leader of the homeless nation, and wrote, "I could have tortured others of your world, but I chose to torture my world, because I preyed on the weak."

Quakenbush described Silveria as being cordial, amiable, having a pleasant manner typical of serial killers, and believes that this allowed him to get close to his victims. Silveria reminds him of Eddie Haskell from the *Leave It to Beaver* show. But Silveria is not a member of the FTRA. In fact, he made a point during his confession that his crimes had nothing to do with the FTRA. There's no doubt that Silveria rode and jungled up with FTRA hobos, but such loose associations are common on the rails and hardly constitute evidence of collusion.

Quakenbush's take on the FTRA is more restrained than that of Officer Grandinetti. In his view, they have the profile of a '50s or '60s biker gang, and though they have no set hierarchy, he suspects there may be powerbrokers among them, "people who can get things done." But he told me it's impossible to get a handle on them because of the anonymity of their lifestyle, which enables them to slide through the system, to move two states down the road in a matter of hours without going through easily surveilled areas such as airports and bus stations. Maybe, he said, there's a pecking order based on seniority, on how long an FTRA member has been riding; but again, it's hard to be sure. My impression of Quakenbush's attitude toward the FTRA is that they're interesting to him from a law enforcement standpoint, but that he's got more pressing matters on his desk.

Madcat's a veteran of Desert Storm, and he's got pictures to prove it. Photographs of him and his buddies dressed in camo and posed with their weapons in the sand. He keeps them wrapped in a small American flag, and uses them like ID. Breaks them out, explains the meaning and circumstances attendant upon each, then packs them up, never to be shown again. I've tried to get him talking about the war, thinking that the reason he's on the rails and homeless must have some relation to his tour of duty. He hasn't told me much. He once described the enormous encampment in the desert where he was billeted, a medium-sized town of lion-colored tents and roaring machinery. One day, he says, he was driving a truck through the desert and came upon a crate of Stinger missiles lying in the middle of nowhere. He thought this was funny until he was ordered to transport them to an arsenal and learned that they were unstable, that a sudden jolt might launch one straight at the back of his head —at least that's what he was told. He drove at 3 mph all the way, and was disciplined for his tardiness.

"Don't matter you got smart bombs," he says, "when all there is, is idiots to drop 'em."

Madcat doesn't talk much about anything in his past. From his accent, I'd guess he's from the south, maybe Texas; the way he says "forward" ("fao-wud") puts me in mind of people I know in Houston. He's average height, skinny, got a touch of gray in his ragged beard. Early thirties, I figure. A sharp, wary face dominated by large grayish blue eyes, the kind of face one sees staring glumly at the camera in Mathew Brady's Civil War photographs. Whenever we've ridden together, he rarely speaks unless I ask him a question. For the most part he stays quietly drunk and plays with dogs belonging to other hobos. Since many FTRA tramps travel with dogs, he's gotten to know quite a few of them.

"They're all right," he says. "You mess with 'em, they'll stand up to you. And there's some you want to be careful around. But you can say the same about a lot of bars you walk into, the people there."

This particular afternoon I'm supposed to meet an FTRA

member known as Erie Flash at Madcat's office, a Seattle tavern that caters to transients. Ranks of pint and half-pint bottles of Thunderbird stand in front of a clouded mirror behind the bar, and the chewed-up leatherette booths are occupied by an assortment of damaged-looking people: an elderly Santa-shaped gentleman with a lumpish, mauve nose; a pair of down-at-heels Afro-Americans; a disheveled middle-aged couple who're having an argument. A chubby Aleut woman in a torn man's shirt and jeans sits at the bar, holding her head in her hands. Madcat's not in the best shape himself. He's nursing a glass of wine, pressing the heel of one hand against his brow; he's been in a fight, and sports a bloody nose and a discolored lump over one eye. Fighting is the most prominent symptom of Madcat's problem. When he's staying in a city, in a squat or a mission, he'll get in a fight a day, sometimes more; he claims that fighting is the only way he "can get the devil out." But when he's riding, it seems that the closeness of the train soothes his particular devil. It's possible, I think, the trains have a similar effect on others, which would explain in part why there's so much sadness out on the rails—some hobos are attracted to the trains because the potency of those 2-million-ton presences and their metal voices act to subsume their pain.

We've been waiting almost an hour when Flash makes his appearance. He's tall, physically imposing, and has a biker intensity that's in line with his reputation as a man with—according to the grapevine—no compunctions about murder. It's said he manufactures speed from starter fluid and drugstore inhalers, among other ingredients, and once he gets cranked up, he's a dangerous person to be around. Under a denim jacket, he's wearing his FTRA colors, a black bandana held in place by two silver conchos. Thick black hair threaded with gray falls to his shoulders. Dark, alert eyes. His hands are large, with prominent knuckles; his features are well-defined, strong, but dissolution has taken a toll, and what I'm seeing now is the ruins of a handsome man. He's been staying with a local woman in her home, and looks healthier than other gang members I've encountered. Like most hobos, he doesn't offer a handshake to someone he's just met.

I tell him I'd like to hear his angle on the FTRA story, and he says fiercely, "I ain't got no damn story. Not one I want you to hear." But after I buy him a pint of T-bird, he seems mollified and takes the stool beside me. As he talks, he has the habit of looking down at his glass and then slowly turning his head toward me, a tight movement, finishing the turn as he finishes his thought—he might be tracking the carriage of an invisible typewriter.

"None of you gave a shit about us before," he says. "We could dry the fuck up and blow away, you wouldn't care. Now some nut case kills a few people, and you're all over us. How'd you like it I come in your house and go to asking a bunch of dumb-ass questions? S'pose I barge into your living room and say, ''S'cuse me, buddy. You always drink two martinis 'fore you screw your girlfriend, or is that just 'cause it's Tuesday?'"

I start to speak, but he cuts me off.

"You got your own nuts you can write about. Ted Bundy and all them other freaks. Sidetrack don't have a damn thing to do with the FTRA." He holds up his empty pint, which he's drained in three gulps—I signal the bartender.

"Sooner or later," he goes on, "one of you shitbrains is gonna piss somebody off and get yourself killed. Then you'll have a fucking story. The rails ain't no place to be asking questions. Hobos want to be left the fuck alone. That's why we're out there. Keep pestering us, we'll let you know about it."

By the time he's started in on his third pint, Flash has completely abandoned his intention of not talking to me, and is taking it upon himself to smarten me up, chump that I am. He's mellowed; his gestures are not so tightly controlled, and his voice has acquired a lazy, gassed quality, causing me to think that his original hostility might have been chemically enhanced.

"People are setting up Eddie Bauer tents in the jungles," he says. "Walking around with scanners and hiking boots. You take a stroll through a place where everybody's starving, and you're packing a bag of groceries, what you expect's gonna happen? The rails is where we live, man. It ain't a fucking theme park. All this shit you're stirring up—" he taps me on the chest "—one of you's gonna wind up eating it. And it ain't because the FTRA is the fucking mafia, y'know. 'Cause it ain't. We take care of our own, but that's as far as it goes."

I ask him if there's a hierarchy in the gang, any structure, and he lets out a scornful laugh.

"You think I kill people, don't you?" he asks. "That's the reason you're talking to me."

The question catches me off guard. "I don't know. Do you?"

He gives me a steady look. "I do what I have to. We all do what we have to, right?"

"I suppose."

"Well, that's exactly what I do . . . what I have to. That's your structure. That's all the structure there is."

"So you're saying it's the survival of the fittest?"

"I'm saying that right here, the three of us—" his gesture includes me and Madcat "—if we're out riding, one of us is president, one's vice president." He grins. "Then there's you."

"If that's all it is, why join a gang?"

"Brotherhood, man. You need me to explain brotherhood to you?"

The Aleut woman a few seats down makes a low keening noise, and Flash regards her with disfavor.

"I got no reason to tell you shit," he says, coming back to me. "I told you some of the things I done, you wouldn't understand 'em. The world you live in, the only excuse there is for killing is self-defense. But where I live there might be a thousand good reasons for killing somebody any given moment. That don't mean you got to enjoy it. But you better be up for it."

I think of men accustomed to killing whom I've spoken to in prison, who've handed me similar bullshit. Every one of them maintained an outlaw bad-to-the-bone stance until they felt they were in a circumstance in which they had nothing to prove, no one to impress; then they revealed a more buoyant side to their natures, brimming over with cheerfulness, their talk rife with homily, as if bloodshed had done wonders for their spirits, as if having crossed over the border of acceptable human conduct, they had been delighted to discover that they had retained their basic sensibilities and not been transformed into a depraved subspecies by the resonance of their crimes. I sense this potential in Flash; though he hasn't dropped his badass pose, I'm certain that in another environment, he'd loosen up and wax anecdotal and analyze himself in terms of a woeful childhood.

"You and me should take a ride sometime," he says. "If you want to get to know somebody, best way is to take a ride with 'em."

He's mocking me, and the only thing I can think to say is, "Yeah, maybe."

"Well, you let me know, huh?" He gets to his feet, digs for his wallet, then remembers that I'm the one paying. He nods to Madcat and says, "Safe rails, brother." And then he's gone.

Madcat is holding his head to one side, a hand still pressed to his brow to alleviate the throbbing of the lump above his eye. I ask if he's okay, and he says, "Pissed off is all."

"Why's that?" I ask, and he says, "The guy who whipped me, he wasn't that big a deal. Guess I ain't as much a man as I used to be."

He seems unreasonably distressed—he's lost fights before. I can't think how to restore his spirits.

"You still up for riding?"

"Oh, yeah. I'll be fine."

But he looks utterly dejected.

I ask if he wants some more wine before we head out, and he says, "Naw, fuck. Wine don't do no good for me."

He stares down into his glass, swirls the liquid around; then lifts his head and turns his gaze to the street, watching the passers-by with a forlorn expression, as if seeing in their brisk movements yet another condemnation of his weakness.

"Wish't I'd had me a bottle of whiskey," he says. "I'd been drinking whiskey, I'd a kicked his ass."

Cricket is 48, a grandmother, and an FTRA member. She once operated a cleaning business in Tucson that catered to restaurants and resorts, but in 1988 she began to feel "stressed out, there was too many things goin' on," and she sold everything she owned and hit the rails—she'd done some riding previously, and she loved the trains. Ever since, she's ridden from town to town, stopping now and then to work, helping build stages for bands in a Spokane hotel, or "hanging a sign" to get house-cleaning jobs. I contact her by phone, and she tells me she's temporarily off the rails due to problems associated with injuries she received in 1994, when two hobos named Pacman and Lone Wolf killed her friend, Joseph Carbaugh, axed her in the head, then threw her and another friend off a moving train near Glenwood Springs, Colorado. Pacman and Lone Wolf are independent hobos, she says, though they claim to be members of a group called the Wrecking Crew. Or maybe it was the Goon Squad—sometimes, she says, she can't remember names, because of her injuries.

"I thought the Wrecking Crew and the Goon Squad were part of the gang," I say, recalling Grandinetti's lecture. "Part of the FTRA."

"Naw, they're separate groups," Cricket says. "But FTRA ain't a gang."

"What is it, then?"

"It's a brotherhood, a sisterhood," she says. "We hold reunions, like high school classes do. We go to reunions, we party, we travel."

I ask if rape was involved in her initiation, or in any other FTRA woman's initiation that she knows of, and she says, "That's bullshit! When I first got with the FTRA, I was a south rider, riding out of Tucson with Santa Claus and some of those guys, and there wasn't no initiation. Then I started going with Diamond Dave, and when we went up north, he got initiated, so I did, too. 'New tits on the tracks,' we call it. All it was, you had to go one-on-one with another chick. I had to sit there and prove I could ride anywhere. That I knew enough to ride. But rape . . . I mean, it happens on the rails sometimes. But it's like everywhere, like in society. It's usually somebody you know. Date rape."

"Did you have to fight during the initiation?"

"Yeah," she says. "Tracy Jean Parker. She was on me pretty good. But that was just her, it wasn't an FTRA thing. Real fights are few and far between."

I ask her about drug running, " . . . drug corridors along the rails from Texas," and she says, "That's not the FTRA . . . or maybe there's one or two. Some of those new little FTRAs, they all got barbed-wire tattoos on their arms. They got different ethics from us. The Hole in the Wall Gang. Montana Brew Crew. Some of them are maybe into that. But the older crew, we get drunk, we cause a commotion. Sometimes chicks'll strip naked or go topless just to get a reaction from a yard master or the bulls. But we don't take it to town.

"You're gonna have a rotten apple or two in every group," she goes on. "Like Sidetrack. I traveled with him, I slept beside him many times. He was always laughing and smiling. It's hard for me to believe he did all that they said."

"Does the FTRA operate safe houses?" I ask.

"There's the missions," she says, sounding a bit puzzled. "God's Love in Helena, and there's one in Pasco. Charity House in Spokane. And when I get to a town and I got friends there, I visit them."

Like others in the FTRA, Cricket has problems with certain of her brothers, Mississippi Bones in particular. "He was a manipulator," she says. "He was always siccin' Misty Jane—that was his wife —onto other women, gettin' her to fight 'em. I seen him get her onto Sweetpea and Snow White and Missy Jones. He cut my rag (took her bandana) one time, but I waited till he passed out and took it back. Everything Bones did was behind drinkin'. He got disgraced soon after that—Chester the Molester took his concho. If F-Trooper cut him, chances are he had a good reason."

I ask if there's anything she wants to get out about the FTRA, and after a pause, she says, "You got no idea how many different kinds of people ride. Carneys. Mexicans and Indians. Religious people. Preachers, people from the Rainbow Gathering. Deadheads. More kinds'n I can think of right now. If any of 'em commit a crime, the cops try and pin it on the FTRA.

"Bein' FTRA don't get you nothin'—not the way people are

sayin'. Your brothers and sisters'll help you out, now. There's a lot of helpin' goin' on out there. One time I'm gettin' married on the tracks in Spokane up close to the Welfare Bridge. Gettin' married to Cherokee. Manny the railroad bull—he's an ordained preacher, he's doin' the ceremony. We didn't have no money for rings, so these two sisters from Helena bought some rings and hopped a train to come all the way up and give 'em to us.

"That was somethin' special. But mostly it's little things. Like when Joshua Longgone lost his dog, and everyone spent hours beatin' the weeds for him. Or when you haven't got money for food, and someone'll hand you over a few dollars. Or when you bring a bottle to someone who's startin' to shake all over, goin' for the DTs, just dyin' for a drink."

The day after New Years, 1998, and I'm at a hobo gathering in New Mexico, maybe a hundred people jungled up on a patch of desert figured by saguaro and mesquite and sage and a big, dark lizardback tumble of rock that sticks up beside a section of Southern Pacific track. Atop the rock, several flags are flying—American, Confederate, MIA, Anarchist. The raising of the Anarchist banner caused a minor dust-up earlier in the day, when one of the encamped riders, said to be a KKK member, objected to its presence; but he's been appeased. He and his family spend a good deal of their time zooming around on motorized all-terrain bikes, making an aggressive show of having fun, and don't mix with the rest of us.

I'm perched on a ledge close to the flags, gazing down on the place. Below and to my left, some elderly hobos are sitting beneath two small shade trees, occupying chairs arranged in a circle around the remains of the previous night's campfire; beyond them, a communal kitchen has been erected, and people are busy cooking hash for breakfast. Farther off, there's a trailer on which helium tanks are mounted; they're used to fill balloons, which now and again can be seen floating off into a clouded pewter sky. Children scoot about, playing and squabbling in the dirt. Tents scattered here and there; vehicles of every description—pickups, campers, old shitboxes. The whole thing calls to mind a scene from a low-budget film about life after some civilization-destroying disaster, the peaceful settlement of the good guys in the moment before the motorized barbarians come swooping down to rape and steal gas. Trains pass with regularity, and when this happens, rockets are set off and people move close to the tracks and wave. The engineers sound their whistles, wave back, and on occasion toss freight schedules from the engine window.

The King of the Hobos, Frog Fortin, an FTRA member whose coronation took place last summer at the hobo convention in Britt, Iowa, was supposed to put in an appearance here, but to my dismay, he's a no-show. The majority of the attendees are railfans, people who've done some hoboing but now have day jobs and families and can't be classified as hobos—they simply love trains. There are also, as mentioned, some old-time hobos, men in their sixties and seventies; and there are staff members of the *Hobo Times,* "America's Journal of Wanderlust," a publication given to printing treacly hobo poetry.

Most of these folks don't feel like talking about the FTRA. Some disparage them, passing them off as drunks who're more likely to harm themselves than anyone else. Others are hostile when I mention the subject. They feel that the FTRA has brought down the heat on all riders, and don't want to contribute to more bad publicity. Most of those who are willing to talk don't have much to add to what I already know, but I meet a photographer who's ridden with the FTRA, who tells me about black FTRA members—New York Slim, the Bushman, et al.—and attributes FTRA racism to the enforced racism inherent in the prison system. It's more habitual, he says, than real. Another rider, Lee, agrees with him, and says that although the FTRA use racist iconography in their tattoos and graffiti, they are "oddly egalitarian racists."

Lee is a 42-year-old wilderness squatter who was involved with the Earth First movement, until he became fed up with the group's internal politics. He lives in a tiny house he built himself in the midst of a redwood forest in Northern California; it's so carefully camouflaged, it's almost impossible to spot from a distance of 15 feet. There he publishes *Hobos from Hell/There's Something About a Train,* a 'zine containing stories about the rails written by a variety of hobos. He's dressed, as is his custom, all in black. Black sweats, black raincoat, black baseball hat. Makes him harder to spot in the yards at night. Though he's no hermit, his face has the sort of mild openness I associate with someone who's spent time in the solitudes. His features are weathered, but his energy and humor make him seem younger than his years. He says he looks forward "to the collapse of the Industrial State," but when that happens, he'll miss the trains. It strikes me that, for Lee, a perfect world would be one in which man has become extinct, the planet has reverted to a natural state, and the only reminders of the human past are the trains, evolved to an inorganic form of life, traveling endlessly across the wild and making their eerie music.

Because I want to talk about the FTRA, Lee decides to take our conversation up to the flags, where no one else will hear. But we wind up talking less about the FTRA than about "the next generation of hobos," one that includes the "crusty punks" and young eco-activist riders. Lee places the latter in the tradition of the Wobblies, who used the rails to spread their political message back in the '30s; he describes them as "goal-oriented, self-educated wanderers." The crusty punks are pierced, tattooed, homeless youth who come out of hardcore squat scenes in urban areas, and are "apolitical, non-racist white trash." A subgroup, the "gutter punks," he likens to the Untouchable class excluded from the Hindus. He expresses concern that these younger riders haven't been accepted by the old hobos, mainly because their rowdy behavior has attracted the attention of the police and thus brought down even more heat. He seems to like them all, has ridden with them, but he's frustrated by the crusties' self-destructiveness. I wonder if his attitude toward them, his compassion, may echo a similar attitude that caused him frustration when he was involved with the Earth Firsters.

That night people gather around the campfire, drinking beer and swapping rail stories. There's SLC, a hobo out of Salt Lake who once owned a mail-order computer company, which he lost to the IRS, and has just spent a month working on a hog farm; there's Dante Faqwa, an old-time hobo; there's Buzz Potter, editor of the *Hobo Times*; there's a lady hobo, Connecticut Shorty; there's a short, truculent guy in his late twenties who calls himself Bad Bob. Lee is there with a couple of friends. Adman is there. Along with many, many others I haven't met. Listening to scraps of conversation, it's possible to believe that I'm in a hobo jungle back during the Depression:

"Is the Sacramento Kid around the fire?"
". . . wasn't a bull for a thousand miles . . ."
". . . it's always been a motherfucker to catch out of . . ."
". . . they closed the mission in Atlanta . . ."
". . . the train didn't go till sundown . . ."
". . . best chicken I ever ate came from that alley . . ."

Whenever a train draws close, fireworks are set off; starbursts flower overhead as the engine approaches the camp, roaring and moaning, flattening the brush with the wind of its passage. Night is the best time to watch trains; they seem grander and more magical. There's a gravity about them you can't feel as strongly in the daylight. They are, I think, kind of like the giant sandworms in *Dune*

. . . of course, it's possible this and all my previous perceptions are colored by the fact that I'm seriously baked. Two monster joints and a bunch of beer. Whatever, I realize that I'm being seduced by all the happy-wanderer, freedom's-just-another-word-for-freight-hopping, hash-cooking, dumpster-diving esprit de poverty that's rising up from these sons and daughters of the iron horse, like heat from Mother Nature's steaming yoni. Which is okay, I suppose. I'll have to turn in my cynic's card, but hey, maybe I've migrated to a better world. Maybe the stars are actually spelling out song lyrics, and the pile of stones shadowing us has turned into the Big Rock Candy Mountain.

Then the singing starts for real. Old broadwater ballads such as "Barbara Allen" delivered by a friend of Lee's whose sweet tenor exhibits signs of academic training. A rider in a bush hat and desert camo hauls out a guitar. In a brief conversation earlier that day, he made violently homophobic comments; but now, with no appreciable acknowledgment of irony, he proceeds to deliver a thoroughly professional rendition of "City of New Orleans," concluding with the reverential statement, "That song was written by Mister Steven Goodman." More train songs follow. The mystical union of the rails is dissolving into a hootenanny. I sense that once all the railroad songs have been exhausted, a few verses of "Where Have All the Flowers Gone" would not be deemed inappropriate.

Adman drops into a chair close by, and says something about "the bluehairs in their RVs," contrasting these conservative seniors and their feeble journeyings with "the wisdom in the eyes of old hobos." His delivery grows increasingly rhapsodic, peaking as he describes how, during one series of rides, his cassette recorder broke and he was forced to scavenge for batteries. "I hooked it up with batteries from a *dumpster*, and I'm listening to *opera*." His voice full of wonderment, as if recounting not long after the event, how the young Arthur Pendragon pulled Excalibur from its imprisoning stone. He's probably as blitzed as I am, but even knowing this, it's hard to bear. The whole scene has become an enormous sugar rush, and I have to get away. I like these people. No matter how dippy this part of their fantasy, the rest of it's way cooler than most. I move out into the darkness, where other refugees from the fire are drinking cups of beer and looking off into the blue shadows of the desert.

Tonight I'm drinking more heavily, sitting on a grassy embankment next to a Portland strip mall with half a dozen crusty punks. They're happy to drink up my money, but only one wants to talk. Her name, she tells me, is Jailbait. She could pass for thirteen, says she's seventeen—if you split the difference, you'd probably be right. Dirty blond hair hangs into her eyes, accentuating her waifish quality. Clean her up, dress her in something besides baggy jeans and a hooded sweatshirt, she'd be breaking ninth grade hearts. A crop of inflamed blemishes straggles across her forehead, so distinct against the pale skin, it makes me think I could connect the dots and come up with a clown's face or a crude map of Rhode Island; and maybe it's only a combination of the malt liquor and the reflection of the neon sign on the roof behind us, but her teeth look kind of green.

Jailbait's been living in a squat with her friends for six weeks, but now it's getting cold, they're thinking about LA or maybe San Diego. She tells me she comes from LA, but I hear the great Midwest in her speech. I ask why she left home, and she looks off into the sky, where stars are sailing clear of a patchy mist, and says without inflection, "It was just fucked up." She's been riding for a year, she says, and she's never had any trouble with the FTRA.

"They yell sex stuff at us sometimes, y'know. But that's about it." She rubs at a freshly inked homemade tat that spreads from the soft area between thumb and forefinger to cover the back of her left hand. I can't make out what it's supposed to be—a blurred network of blue-black lines—but I'm fairly certain the tiny scabs at the center are tracks.

"We don't hang out with them much," she goes on. "Some of them are cool, I guess. There's one I met last summer played the harmonica. He was nice. But most of 'em, they're these old fucked-up guys, y'know."

"They never got aggressive with you?"

"Carter got chased by them once." She glances up at her friends, who're sitting above us on the slope, and addresses a sullen, muscular kid with the basic Road Warrior look: stubbly scalp, heavy designwork on his neck and arms, and enough cheap facial jewelry to set off an airport detector. "Wasn't those guys chased you back in Pasco FTRA?"

Carter shrugs, takes a hit off his forty.

"He stole some of their shit," Jailbait says. "But they couldn't catch him."

"I didn't steal nothin'," says Carter. "I was just walkin' past and this ol' fuck started waving a knife."

"If you didn't steal nothin', you were thinkin' about it." This from a chunky blond girl in a tight turtleneck and a stained black mini and torn stockings. Her make-up's so thick, it reminds me of Kabuki.

"Fuck you!" says Carter.

The girl's voice grows querulous. "You know you were! You said you were gonna see if they had any wine!"

Carter jumps to his feet and makes as if to backhand her. He goes off on her, shouting, his face contorted with anger, using the C word with frequency. He's sick of her skanky hole, why doesn't she just fucking die.

The girl turns her head away, holds up an arm to ward off a blow; she's crying, cursing him softly. The other three boys—less flamboyantly accessorized versions of the Carter doll—laugh and do some high-fiving.

"C'mon, Carter," says Jailbait. "Don't be an asshole."

It was as if a switch had been triggered in Carter's brain, releasing an icy fluid. He grows calm, mutters a final word of warning, and sits back down. The chunky girl lifts her head and glares at Jailbait.

It doesn't matter what sort of question I ask the crusties, I realize. I could ask about their favorite TV show and tap into the same group dynamic, the same pattern of sullenness evolving into fury, then lapsing into drunken silence. I'm curious about them, but they're impervious to curiosity. They're floating on some terminal wavelength that's beaming the length and breadth of the country, controlling them as they slide from exotic chemical peaks to troughs of low self-esteem. Another tragic cliché being woven into the decaying electric tapestry of the times.

I tell them I have to go; I'm hoping to catch out from the switchyard across the river in Vancouver, Washington, in a couple of hours; the guy I'm riding with says they're putting together an eastbound.

"That's a pussy yard," Carter says, giving me a challenging stare; it's the first time he's spoken directly to me for an hour. "Fuckin' old lady could catch out of Vancouver."

A babble erupts from the other boys—they're throwing out the names of various yards, ranking them according to degree of difficulty. Vidalia's no problem. Likewise Dilworth. The bulls at Klamath Falls have gotten nasty. Salt Lake City's not too bad, except for all the pedophiles.

"You think you know something, don't you?" Carter says. "You got it all figured out."

This confuses me. I can't decide if Carter's smarter than he looks, if he has a sense of what I'm thinking, or if this is just another bellicose twitch. I'd prefer to believe the former—it would be nice to be surprised.

"Figured what out?"

Carter comes up into a half-crouch, balanced on one hand; he's trying to look menacing, doing a decent job of it. "Fuck you," he says.

I'm almost drunk enough to respond. Carter doesn't really want to fight, though I'm sure he could get into it; he just wants to win the moment—it's all he's got worth risking a fight over. Could be he's a rotten kid and deserves his crummy life. But I don't need to make things worse for him. Nor am I eager to have him and his pals dance on my head.

The six of them straggle up the embankment, away from me. Five of them at the crest, silhouetted against the backdrop of the convenience store. It looked as if the neon sign were the sky and the drugged, lost children were the newly aligned constellations of a hellish American midnight zodiac, and that Carter, stationed slightly below the rest, staring bitterly back at me, was the rising sign.

Madcat and I are somewhere in Montana, I think. One of those little prairie towns that at night show like a minor cluster of stars too disorganized to suggest a clever shape. The train has stopped, but I can't see any signs from where we're resting, just low, unlit buildings and a scrap yard. I'd ask Madcat, but he's asleep. We're sitting on the rear porchlike section of a grain car, bundled up against the early morning chill, and I worry about whether we should get off and hide in the weeds in case they check the cars. Then the train lurches forward, and we're rolling again. As we gather speed I spot two men jogging along the tracks behind us, trying for another car. In the electric blue of the predawn darkness, they're barely more than shadows, but I have an impression of raggedness, and I'm pretty sure one has a bushy beard. FTRA, I think. Officer Grandinetti is right, he just hasn't taken his vision of the gang far enough. The FTRA are everywhere. Mystical, interpenetrating, sinister. I've asked one too many questions, and from his fastness deep in the Bitterroots, the criminal mastermind Daniel Boone has focused his monstrous intellect upon me, sent thought like a beam of fire from a crystal to sting the minds of his assassins and direct them to me.

A cold-looking smear of yellow light seeps up from the horizon, the gunmetal blue of the sky begins to pale, and the day reveals rolling wheat fields and a tiny reservation town of trailers and rusted pickups standing a quarter-mile or so from the tracks. It's an ordinary sight made extraordinary by my vantage: tired, dirty, and illegal, sitting inside the roar of the train, in the midst of the solitudes, living a moment available to no one else, the shimmer of the wheat, clouds with silver edges and blue-gray weather heavy in their bellies pushing in low from the north, and the abandoned look of the trailers, discolored siding and sprung doors, one pitched at an angle, come off its blocks, and watchful crows perched along a fence line like punctuation—it's all infused with a sense of urgent newness, the mealy blight of the ordinary washed away. Maybe, I think, this is something I should be homesick for, something I should pursue. But then I recall Mississippi Bones walking away at the end of our interview in the prison at Florence, leaning on his cane, a guard at his side. Halfway across the room he turned back and stared at me. In retrospect, I believe he may have been making a judgment as to whether it was worthwhile to offer me advice. When he did speak, his tone was friendly yet cautionary, like that of someone telling a child not to play in the street.

"Stay off the trains," he said.

Over Yonder

*I*T WAS A BLACK TRAIN CARRIED BILLY LONG
Gone away from Klamath Falls and into the east. Away from
life itself, some might say. And if you were to hear the stories of
those who watched it pass, you'd have to give credence to that
possibility . . . though you'd be wise to temper your judgment, considering the character of the witnesses. Three hobos drunk on
fortified wine, violent men with shot livers and enfeebled hearts and
leaky imaginations who lived on the wild edge of nothing and were
likely half-expecting their own black train to pass. Every car was
unlettered, they'd tell you. No corporate logos, no mention of
Union Pacific or Burlington Northern, no spray-painted graffiti.
And the engine wasn't a squatty little unit like they stick on freights
front and back nowadays, it was the very image of the old Streamliner engines, but dead black instead of silver. The sort of train
rumored to streak through small American towns in the four o'clock
dark with a cargo of dead aliens or parts of a wrecked spacecraft,
bound for Roswell or points of even more speculative military purpose. But all this particular train carried was Billy and the big man
in a wide-brimmed hat who had stolen his dog, Stupid.

You could scarcely ever tell when Billy Long Gone was mad,
because he looked mad all the time. If you had caught sight of him
that night, stomping along the tracks with his shoulders bowed

under his pack, breath steaming in the cold, his eyes burning out from tangles of raggedy graying hair and beard, regular Manson lamps framed by heavy ridges and cheekbones so sharp, they like to punch through the skin, you'd have sworn he was the Badass King of the Hobos come to pay his disrespects. But truth is, Billy was rarely mad. All the glare and tension in his face that people took for anger was just a feverish wattage of weakness and fear. He was an anxious little man. Anxious about everything. About if he had money to buy sufficient wine to keep his head right, or if it was going to rain, or what was that noise out in the weeds, and was the freight schedule he'd gotten off the bull in Dilworth the real thing . . . or had the bull just been fucking with him? Nights when he got talky high on cheap greasy speed cooked up from starter fluid and sinus remedies, he'd try to explain where all that anxiety came from. He'd tell himself and anybody else within earshot a lie about a girl and a shit job and some money gone missing and him getting blamed for it. A lie, I say. The details simply didn't hang together, and everything that had happened to him was someone else's fault. But his friends knew it was standing in for another story hidden deep in the addled, short-circuited mess he'd made of his brain, something not so dramatic, something he'd juiced up to make himself feel better, something he couldn't help living inside no matter how much wine or crank he buried it under, and that one was probably not a lie.

Now you'd do better coming between a man and his wife than you would stealing a tramp's dog. It's a relationship where the thought of divorce never enters in, a bond sealed in the coldest cracks of winter and the loneliest squats in Godforsakenland. Steal a tramp's dog, you might be stealing the one thing that's keeping him walking and above ground. So while Billy was mad some that night, he was mostly shaken up. He couldn't figure why Stupid, a slobbery none-too-bright black Lab mix with small tolerance for strangers, had gone and trotted off with his abductor, wagging his tail and never a backward glance—that's how the three hobos he'd been jungled up with described what happened while he was off fetching wine from the ShopRite. He had no reason to doubt them, drunks though they were. Neither did he doubt that they had, as they claimed, tried to stop the man, but couldn't handle him because of his size. "Big as goddamn Hulk Hogan" was the phrase that one communicated to Billy. He loosened the ax handle he kept stowed in his pack, but he had no clear idea what he would do if he found the man.

The train was stopped on a siding outside the Klamath Falls switchyard, a stretch of track that ran straight as an avenue between ranks of tall spruce, and as Billy walked alongside it, peering into the open boxcars, he noticed a number of peculiarities. The walls of the cars were cold to the touch, yet not so cold as you'd expect steel to be on a chilly night, and they were unnaturally smooth. Not a scrape, a ding, or a dent. The only imperfection Billy observed was a long ridged mark like an old scar running across the door of one. As for the doors themselves, they had no locks, and while mounted in the usual fashion, they moved soundlessly, easily, and seemed fabricated of a metal considerably lighter and less reflective than steel—a three-quarter moon hanging overhead cast a silvery shine onto the tops of the rails, but the surfaces of the boxcars gave back scarcely a glimmer. Then, too, the damn thing didn't smell like a train. No stink of refried diesel and spilled cargoes and treated wood. Instead, there was a faint musky odor, almost sweet, as if the entire string of cars had been doused with perfume. Ordinarily, Billy would have been spooked by these incongruities, but he was so worked up about his dog, he ignored the beeping of his interior alarm and kept on walking the tracks.

A stiff breeze kicked up, drawing ghostly vowels from the boughs, and the spruce tops wobbled, then tipped all to one side, like huge drunken dark green soldiers with pointy hats, causing Billy to feel alone among the mighty. He knew himself a tiny figure trudging through the ass-end of nothing beside a weird mile-long something that resembled a train but maybe wasn't, far from the boozy coziness of his fire and his friends, spied on by the moon, the stars, and all the mysterious shapes that lived behind them. It minded him of an illustration in a children's book he'd looked at recently—a pale boy with round eyes lost in a forest where the shadows were crookedly, sinisterly different in shape from the limbs and leaf sprays that cast them. It comforted Billy to think of this picture; it gave him a place to go with his fear, letting him pretend he was afraid instead of *being* afraid. He spent a lot of his time hiding out in the third person this way, objectifying the moments that upset him, especially when he was frightened or when he believed people were talking against him, whispering lies he couldn't quite catch (this is why I'm telling the story like I am now, and not like I will later on when I relate how it was for me after things changed). So when he spotted Stupid poking his head out the door of the next boxcar, his heart was made suddenly, unreservedly, childishly glad, and he went forward in a shuffling run, hobbled by the weight of his pack. Stupid disappeared back into the car and by the time Billy reached the door, he couldn't make out anything inside. The edge of his fear ripped away the flimsy shield of his imagination. He yanked out his ax handle and *swooshed* it through the air.

"Stupid!" he called. "Come on, boy!"

Stupid made a happy noise in his throat, but stayed hidden, and —to Billy's surprise—another dog with a deeper bark went *woof.* Then a man's voice, surprisingly mild, said, "Your dog's comin' with me, friend."

"Hell you say!" Billy swung his ax handle against the door and was startled—the noise was not the expected clang but a dull *thwack* such as might have resulted from hitting a sofa cushion with a two-by-four.

"You send him on out!" Billy said. "I ain't fuckin' with ya!"

"I got no leash on him," the man said.

Billy peered into the car and thought he spied a shadowy figure against the rear wall. He whistled and Stupid made another throaty response, but this one sounded confused. "Son of a bitch! Fuck you done with my dog?" Billy shouted.

A third dog—part terrier by the sound—let out a high-pitched rip of a growl. Paws clittered on the floor of the car.

"Tell you what, friend," said the man. "Ain't a thing I can do 'bout your dog. Dog's in charge of where he's headed. But I don't mind too much you want to ride along."

These words bred a cold vacancy in Billy's gut and his legs went a little weak. Broke-brained as he was, he knew that taking a train ride with a giant in a pitch-dark boxcar was not the solution to any reasonable problem; but he couldn't figure what else to do. A throbbing, rumbling noise started up. It didn't have the belly-full-of-grinding-bones fullness of a real diesel engine, but an engine's what it must have been, because a shuddery vibration shook the car, and the train jerked forward a couple of feet.

"Best hop on if you comin'," said the man inside the car.

Billy glanced around to see if maybe a bull or somebody else official was nearby. It wasn't in his nature to be running the yard cops in on anyone, especially a fellow tramp, but these were extreme circumstances. No one was in sight, though. Nothing but a bunch of cold dark and lonesome. The train lurched forward again, and this time it started rolling. All the dogs inside the car— Billy thought he could hear a half-dozen separate voices—got to yipping and woofing, as if excited to be going somewhere. The train began to roll faster.

Billy knew he had only seconds before he would no longer be able to keep up, before he'd lose his dog for sure. Desperation spiked in him, driving down his fear. With a shout he shucked his pack, heaved it into the car, then hauled himself in after it. As he lurched to his feet, ready to fight, the train lurched heavily and he went off balance, his arms windmilling, and rammed headfirst into the end wall of the car, knocking himself senseless.

Billy woke to find Stupid licking his face. The drool strings hanging from the dog's dewlaps flicked across his cheek and chin. He pushed Stupid away and sat up holding his head, which was gonging something fierce.

"Welcome aboard, friend," said the man's voice. Billy swiveled his neck around toward him, a movement that caused him to wince.

Flanked by four mongrels, the man was sitting against the far wall. His stretched-out legs seemed to reach halfway across the car, and his shoulders were Frankenstein-sized under the Army surplus poncho he was wearing. He was in better health than any hobos of Billy's acquaintance. His shoulder length hair was dark and shiny, his eyes clear, and his horsy face unmarked by gin blossoms or spider veins or any other sign of ill-use. An ugly face, albeit an amiable one. He had a calmness about him that rankled Billy, who could barely recall what calm was like.

"I ain't your goddamn friend." Billy rubbed his neck, trying to ease a feeling of compression.

"Guess not," said the man. "But I'm bettin' you will be."

The dogs gazed at Billy with the same casual indifference as that displayed by the man, as if they were his familiars. They were a sorry bunch: a scrawny German shepherd; a runty collie with a weepy right eye; a brindled hound with orange eyes and a crooked hind leg; and a stubby-legged gray mutt with a broad chest that, Billy thought, had probably been responsible for the yappy growl. Not a one looked worth the effort it would take to keep them fed and healthy, and Billy speculated that maybe the man suffered from a condition similar to the one that had troubled his old traveling companion Clueless Joe, who had tried to persuade a railroad bull in Yakima to marry him and his dog.

A couple of other things struck Billy as odd. First off, the train had to be traveling forty miles an hour, enough speed so that the sound of their passage should have been deafening; yet they weren't yelling, they were speaking in normal tones of voice. And then there was a faint yellow light inside the car, like the faded illumination that comes during a brownout. The light had no apparent source.

Spooked, Billy spotted the ax handle lying on the floor and grabbed it up. The collie came to his feet and barked, but the big man gentled him, and the dog curled up with the other three once again. Stupid, who had lifted his head, sighed and rested his muzzle on Billy's knee.

"What sorta train is this?" Billy demanded, and the man said:

"Guess you could say we caught us a hot shot. We'll be goin' straight through. No stops."

"Straight through to where?"

"Over yonder," said the man. "You gon' love it."

The train swung into a bend, and in the strong moonlight Billy saw they were moving among a chain of snow peaks that swept off toward the horizon, all with dark skirts of evergreen. The Canadian Rockies, maybe?

"How long was I out for?" Billy asked. "Where the hell are we?"

"'Bout ten, fifteen minutes." The man shifted and the dogs perked up their ears and cut their eyes toward him. "My name's Pieczynski, by the way. Folks call me Pie."

"Bullshit . . . ten minutes! Ain't no country like this ten minutes out of Klamath Falls."

"Sure there is," said the man. "You just never rode it before."

Billy noticed another unsettling thing. It was warmish in the car. An October night at altitude, he should be shivering like a wet cat. He'd squeeze himself into his mummy sack, then wedge the sack into the sleeping bag, and he'd still be cold. A terrible thought, the sort he usually dismissed as the result of too much drink, sprouted in his brain and sent out roots into every fissure, replacing his fear of getting thrown out of the car with a deeper, more soul-afflicting fear.

"What's goin' on here?" he said. "What happened to me?"

The man seemed to be assessing Billy, gauging his quality.

"Was it my liver?" Billy said. "My liver give out? Somebody bust my head open? What was it?"

"You ain't dead, that's what you goin' on about," said the man. "Dead's what you almost was. Alive's what's in front of you."

What with the wine he'd consumed and the blow to his head, Billy's mind worked even less efficiently than normal, and he was coming to view the man as a spirit guide of some sort, one sent to escort him to his eternal torment.

"Okay," he said. "I hear what you're sayin'. But if I was . . . if I's back in the yard and I could see myself now, I'd think I was dead, wouldn't I?"

"Who the hell knows what you'd be thinkin', all the wine you got in ya." The man shoved the mutt's behind off his hat brim and jammed the hat onto his head—it was fashioned out of beige leather and shaped cowboy-style, with the brim turned down in front and the crown hand-notched. "Whyn't you get some sleep? It all be a lot clearer come mornin'."

The floor was softer than any floor Billy had ever run across in a boxcar—that and the warmth made the notion of sleep inviting. But he had the idea that if he went to sleep, he would not wake up happy. "Fuck sleep!" he said. "I want you to tell me what's goin' on!"

"You do what ya feel, friend. But I'm gonna close my eyes for a while." The man turned onto his side and went to patting a stuffed cloth sack—one of three he had with him—into a pillow. He glanced over at Billy and said, "What's your name?"

"You know damn well what's my name! You the one sent to bring me."

The man grimaced. "What is it? Ashcan Ike? The Philadelphia Fuck-up . . . some shit like that?"

Billy told him.

"Billy Long Gone," said the man. "Huh! You sure got the right moniker to be catchin' this particular ride." He settled on his pillow, pushed the hat down over his eyes. "Maybe tomorrow you'll feel good enough to tell me your real name."

An hour or so after the big man started snoring, the train snaked down out of the mountains and onto a marshy plain that put Billy in mind of an illustration in a pop-up dinosaur book he'd found in a Seattle dumpster six months back. It had depicted a marsh that extended from horizon to horizon. Reeds and grass and winding waterways, with here and there a patch of solid ground from which sprung weird-looking trees. Giant dragonflies hovered and flashed in the light, and toothy amphibians poked their wrinkled snouts out of the water. Larger amphibians waded about on their hind legs. There had been over forty different types of dinosaur in the picture —he'd counted every one. Take away the dinosaurs, the dragonflies, and what was left wouldn't be much different from the moonlit plain then passing before his eyes.

The similarity between picture and reality seized hold of him, rerouting his thoughts into a wet-brained nostalgia that induced him to stare open-mouthed at the landscape as if entranced. Scenes from his life melted up from nowhere like skin showing through a soaked T-shirt, then dried away into nothing. Scenes that were part fantasy, part distorted memory, filled with parental taunts, the complaints of women, and the babble of shadowy unrecognizable figures who went tumbling slowly away, growing so small they seemed characters in another alphabet he had never learned to read. Even when the plain was blotted out by the black rush of another train running alongside them, he barely registered the event, adrift in a sodden unfocused delirium. . . . A dog barking brought him halfway back. The brindled hound was standing at the edge of the open door, barking so fiercely at the other train, ropy twists of saliva were slung from its muzzle. All the dogs were barking, he realized. He picked out Stupid's angry, bassy note in the chorus. Then he was snatched up, shaken, and that brought him the rest of the way back. He found himself staring into the big man's frowning face, heard him say, "You with me, Billy? Wake up!" The man shook him again, and he put out a hand in a feeble attempt to interrupt the process.

"I'm here," Billy said. "I'm okay, I'm here."

"Stay back from the door," the man said. "Probably nothin's gonna happen. But just you stay away from it."

The dogs were going crazy, barking at the other train, which was running along a track some thirty feet away, going in the same direction they were, and seemed identical to the train they were riding, with a string of boxcars towed behind a Streamliner engine. Laying tracks so far apart didn't make much sense to Billy, and he was all set to ask the big man how come this was, when something wide and dark fluttered down out of the night sky and settled onto one of the cars. It was as if a dirty blanket had come flapping out of nowhere and collected atop the car in a lump.

Billy thought what he'd seen must have been produced by a defect of mind, a rip in his vision; but before he could refine this thought into opinion, the lump atop the car flared like a sail filling with wind, and he recognized it for a creature of sorts—a rippling, leathery sail-like thing that resembled a manta ray without a tail. Twenty feet across if it was an inch and fringed with cruel, hooked claws. There was an irregular gray splotch at the center from which was extruded the debased caricature of a human head, a bald monstrosity with a mottled scalp, sunken eyes, and a leering, fanged mouth. The thing held aloft for a handful of seconds, then folded into the shape that reminded Billy of a taco shell, funneling the wind away, and sank down once again onto the car, which immediately began to twist and shudder beneath it, making Billy think of a train in an old black-and-white Disney cartoon that had danced along the tracks to Dixieland jazz. Rivulets of glowing yellow fluid spilled out from beneath the creature's edges, flowing down the side of the boxcar, and the roof of the car arched upward, bucking convulsively, the way a cat's back twitches when you tickle it. The assaulted train gave a high-pitched shriek that didn't have the sound of any train horn or whistle with which Billy was familiar, and appeared to scoot forward, starting to pull away from Billy's train. And then the creature raised up again, its body belling. It released the last of its hooks, and the wind took it in rippling flight past the open car where Billy stood gaping, passing close enough so it seemed that ugly little head stared at him with a pair of glittering black eyes and a mouth full of golden juice in the instant before it vanished.

Billy hadn't been afraid while the creature was attacking the train. It had been too compelling a sight. But now he was afraid— now he put what had happened together with all the other strange things he had experienced, and the whole made a terrifying shape in his mind. He glanced at the big man, who was in the process of fluffing up his pillow sack again. The dogs, quiet now, were watching him attentively.

"Call them things 'beardsleys'," the big man said, when he registered Billy's bewilderment. "Friend of mine name of Ed Rogan was the one started callin' 'em that. They used to call 'em somethin' else, but he changed it. Said they reminded him of his eighth grade math teacher. Fella named Beardsley." He gave the sack a final pat and lay back. "They ain't so bad. Hardly ever take more'n a few pints. You'll see worse where you're goin'." He closed his eyes, then cocked one open toward Billy. "Bet you might just know ol' Ed. He useta ride the northern line like you. Called hisself Diamond Dave."

"People been sayin' Diamond Dave's dead. Ain't nobody seen him 'round for years."

"He's doin' right well for a dead guy." The big man shifted about until he got comfortable. "Best thing you can do is get some sleep. I know you got questions, but what I'm gon' tell you's gonna go down a lot easier tomorrow."

If the man hadn't gone right off to sleep, Billy might have told him that he had no questions, he knew he was traveling east through the land of the dead, on his way to whatever hellish corner of it had been prepared for his eternity. No other explanation fit. It would have been nice, he thought, if death had taken away the pain in his lower back and cured his sciatica; but he supposed—like the man said—there would be worse to come.

He shuffled over to where he'd tossed his pack and sat with his back to the end wall. Stupid ambled up, plopped down next to him, and Billy pulled a wadded-up bandanna from his pocket and cleared away some of the saliva from the dog's muzzle. "Dumbass," he said affectionately. "What you think you gon' do, you got at that damn thing? Motherfucker woulda wrapped you up and took you home for a snack." It occurred to him then that if he was dead, Stupid must be dead, too. That pissed him off. The bastards had no right to go tormenting his dog. This so troubled him, his eyes teared and he began feeling sorry for his dead self. He dug into his pack and hauled out a pint of Iron Horse. Unscrewed the cap and sucked down a jolt. Most of the wine went into his stomach before he could taste it, but what he did taste he spat back out.

"Jesus . . . fuck!" He sniffed the neck of the bottle. It smelled horrible. Something must have gone wrong with the batch. It was his last pint, too. He'd wind up drinking it anyway, but for now he didn't want to put up with having to puke. He was wore down, the borders of his consciousness crumbly and vague, like he was coming down from crank. He scrunched himself up to fit the floor and rolled onto his side. Set the pint by his head. The gentle rocking of the train made it seem that the fire-breathing stallion on the label was charging directly into his eyes.

When I woke the next morning, my eyes fell to that same label, but instead of reaching for the bottle in desperate need as I would have the day before, I had a flashback to my last mouthful of Iron Horse and turned away, coming face to face with Stupid, who licked my lips and nose. I got to my feet, feeling less achy than I might have expected. And hungry. That was odd. It had been ten years easy since I woke up wanting breakfast. Pieczynski was still asleep, encircled by the other dogs. I supposed now that he had stolen them all. He was one butt-ugly son of a bitch. That long nose had been flattened and spread, probably by bottles and fists, until it resembled a nose guard on an ancient gladiator's helmet; and his mouth, thick-lipped and wide, bracketed by chiseled lines, made me think of the time my dad had taken me bass fishing, the part before he'd gotten drunk and decided it would be funny to use me as the target for his casts.

Maybe I *was* dead, I thought. I didn't see any other way to explain how I'd felt so bad every single day for the last three, four years, and then, after one night's sleep, it was like I'd never had a drink in my life. And it wasn't only a sense of physical well-being. I felt strong in my head. My thoughts were clear, solid, defined. Even though it had only been seven or eight hours, I was already starting to perceive the Billy Long Gone of the previous night as a different person, the way you might reflect on how you behaved when you were a kid. But I wasn't sure what to think about what I had seen, whether the "beardsley" had been part of an alcoholic fugue or if it had some basis in reality.

I pushed two fingers hard against the wall of the car and felt a slight resilience. Like pushing against stiff leather. I wondered if I was to cut the surface, would glowing yellow blood spurt forth? That could explain the light that illuminated the car. And the warmth. I dug a jackknife out of my jeans pocket, opened the blade, and laid the edge against the black surface; then I thought better of it. I didn't want this particular car to go to twitching and heaving itself around. I folded the knife and put an ear flat to the wall. No pulse I could hear, but I thought I could detect a faint stirring and that caused me to pull my head back in a hurry. The idea of a live train didn't rattle me all that much, though. Hell, I'd always thought of trains as being half-alive anyway. A spirit locked into the steel.

I went to the door of the boxcar and sat gazing out at the land, wishing I had something to eat. We had left the marshes behind and were rolling through a series of hills with long, gradual western slopes and steep drop-offs on their eastern sides, as if they were ancient access ramps of some long-demolished freeway that had been overgrown with tall grasses. The sky was a clear, deep blue with a continent of massy white cloud bubbling up from the northern horizon. Up ahead were bigger hills, dark green in color, lush-looking. The air was soft and pleasantly cool, the air of a spring morning. I took off my shirt to enjoy it; in doing so, I caught a whiff of my body odor. No wonder Stupid was always licking me—I smelled like something two days dead.

"Hungry?" said Pieczynski—his voice startled me, and I nearly toppled out the door. He was holding out what looked to be a flat gray cake with a faint purplish cast.

"What is it?" The cake was cold and slimy to the touch.

"Jungleberries." Pieczynski settled beside me, his legs dangling off the edge of the car. "We mush 'em up and press 'em. Go on . . . give it a try."

I nibbled at the edge of the cake. It was almost tasteless—just a vague fruity tang. I took a bigger bite, then another, then wolfed the whole thing down. It didn't satisfy my hunger, but after a few minutes I felt an appreciable sense of well-being.

"There some kinda dope in this shit?" I asked, taking a second cake from Pieczynski.

He shrugged. "Seein' how they make you feel, I s'pose there must be somethin' in 'em. Couldn't tell you what."

"I don't believe I ever heard of jungleberries." I turned the cake over in my hand, as if expecting to find a list of ingredients.

"There's a whole buncha things you ain't heard of that you're gon' be comin' up against real soon." Pieczynski scrunched around so he could look directly at me. "How you feelin'?"

I gestured with the cake. "Big as you are, I eat another of these damn things, I'm liable to be lookin' down at you."

Pieczynski gave a dismissive flip of his hand. "I ain't talking 'bout if you high. Is your body strong? Your thinkin'? I know they are. Same thing happened to me. Night I crawled onto one of these here trains, I was more messed up than you was. Sicker'n a caught fish from crack. Couldn't keep nothin' in my stomach. Doubt I weighed more'n hunnerd-sixty. I was havin' hallucinations. Truth be told, I was damn near dead. But the next mornin' it was like I was reborn." He took a bite of his cake, chewed it noisily, swallowed. "Same thing happens to ever'body catches out on the black trains."

We had begun climbing a fairly steep grade that would, I supposed, take us up into those dark green hills, and as we passed a defile, I saw at the bottom of it what appeared to be the wreckage of a train like the one we were riding. It was nearly shrouded by huge ferns and other growth, but I made out rips and gouges in the sides of the cars.

"Ever' once in a while comes a flock of beardsleys," Pieczynski said, staring gloomily down at the wreck. "Train ain't gon' survive that."

Despite the cake-and-a-half I'd eaten, the sight of the wreck unsettled me. "What kind of place is this? These things . . . the trains. They're alive, ain't they?"

"They 'bout the most alive things I ever run across. Though that don't seem real plausible if you think about it in terms of where you useta be." Pieczynski spat a gray wad of jungleberry out the door. "Don't nobody know what kind of place this is. Somewheres else is all I know. People taken to callin' it Yonder."

"Somewhere else," I said thoughtfully. "Yonder. That sure 'nough covers a lot of ground."

"Yeah, well. Maybe if some scientist or somebody was here, maybe they could say it better 'bout where we at. But so far ain't nobody caught the ride 'cept for tramps and some kids and a coupla yuppie riders. One of the kid's got hisself a theory about it all, but what he says sounds harebrained to me." Pieczynski made a noise like a horse blowing out breath. "Me, I love it. Life I'm leadin' now beats hell outa the life I useta have. But there's times it don't seem natural. You got these trains rollin' ever'where on tracks nobody built. Ain't even tracks, really. Some sort of natural formation looks like tracks. That ain't weird enough, you got the beardsleys and other animals just as bad. And then you got no people that was born here. It's like God was building a world and decided he didn't like how it was shapin' up, so he went and left it unfinished. I don't know." He tossed a piece of jungleberry cake to the dogs, who sniffed at it and let it lie. "Why should creation be all one way?" he went on. "Why should this place make sense when you lay it next to the one we put behind us? I just leave it at that."

"I think we're dead," I told him. "And this here's the afterlife."

"An afterlife designed for a few hunnerd train riders? Who knows? Maybe. Most ever'body feels they must be dead when they come. But there's one argument against that notion that's tough to get around."

"Oh, yeah? What is it?"

"You can die here, friend," said Pieczynski. "You can die here quicker'n you'd believe."

I asked Pieczynski more questions, but he acted as if talking exhausted him and his answers grew even less informative. I did get out of him that we were headed for a settlement up in the hills, also called Yonder, and that dogs weren't native to this place; he often returned to the world and collected dogs, because they were useful in chasing something he called "fritters" away from the settlement. We fell silent a while and watched the hills build around us, the dark green resolving into dense tropical-looking vegetation. Plants with enormous rain-catching leaves and trees laden with vines and large blue and purple flowers hanging from them in bunches. I spotted dark shapes crossing the sky from time to time, but they were too distant to identify. Every unfamiliar thing I saw disturbed me. Though I still felt good, I couldn't shake a sense of unease. I was certain there was something Pieczynski wasn't telling me, or else there was something important he didn't know. But I'd been considerably more confused about my whereabouts and destination in the past, hopping freights in a state of derangement and winding up in places that it had taken days to locate on my mental map. I had learned to thrive on disorientation. You might say I'd been in training for this kind of ride all my years on the rails.

Pieczynski nodded off for a bit, and I became concerned that we'd sleep past where we were supposed to detrain, so I woke him.

"Jesus Christ!" he said, disgruntled, and rubbed his eyes. He yawned. "Don't worry about it. Train always stops the same places. Always stops in Klamath Falls, always stops in Yonder. That's why they built the settlement there."

"Why's that?"

"Why's it always stop where it does? That what you're askin'?"

"Yeah."

"Y'know, I still ain't figured out how to ask the trains any questions," he said. "Maybe you can figure it out, you ask so many damn questions yourself."

I apologized for waking him, and, mollified, he said it was no big deal. He grabbed a canteen from his pack, had a swallow, and passed it to me. Warmish water. It tasted good.

"You gon' tell me your real name?" he asked. "If I'm gonna introduce you 'round, be better if I knew what to call you."

"Maurice," I said. "Maurice Showalter."

He tried it out, frowned and said, "Damn if I don't believe you be better off stickin' with Billy Long Gone."

The train slowed and stopped, coiled around the base of a hill. We jumped out and started up the slope, pushing through dense brush, bushes with big floppy leaves that spilled water on us as we knocked them aside. From the top of the hill you could see eastward across another expanse of plain scattered about with bright blue lakes shaped roughly like the punctuation to an unwritten paragraph — stray periods, semicolons, and question marks strewn across an immense yellowish green page. Farther off was an area of dark mist that spread along the horizon, broken its entire length by a range of forbidding-looking mountains about ten sizes bigger than the ones we had passed through after leaving Klamath Falls, their peaks set so close together, they might have been a graph forecasting the progress of a spectacularly erratic business. When I asked Pieczynski what lay beyond them, he said he didn't know, he had only traveled a short ways out onto the plain, pointing out an area marked by three small round lakes that formed an elision to an invisible sentence that had no formal ending but simply trailed away . . .

"Call them mountains over there Yonder's Wall," he said. "The trains go up into 'em, and we've had some folks take a ride out that way. Ain't a'one come back to see us." He squinted into the gray distance. "Don't seem like much of an argument for followin' 'em."

We walked along a ridge line for a while, then along a red dirt path that angled down through jungly growth. The dogs trotted ahead and behind us, sniffing at leaves and crawling things, their ears pricking to variations in the fizzing noises—insects, I assumed —that issued from the vegetation. After about five minutes of down, the path leveled off and meandered alongside a rivercourse; I could hear though not see the movement of water close by. Many of the smaller tree trunks were sheathed in a mosaic scale of pale blue and dull green that appeared itself coated in a cracked glaze—glittering wherever the sun struck it. The leaves that dangled down over our heads were tattered and fleshy, like pale green, flabby, boneless hands. Vines were interwoven so thickly above, I couldn't tell if the leaves belonged to a tree or were part of some parasitic growth. Sunlight fell through chinks in the canopy, painting streaks of gold on the path. You could see only about a dozen feet into the jungle on either side before your eye met with an impenetrable wall of growth, and I couldn't understand how, with only two, three hundred people living in Yonder, they kept the path so clear. I'd never been in a tropical jungle before, but I had the thought that it should be hotter and smellier than this one. It still felt like a spring day, and though now and again I caught a hint of rot, the predominant scent was a heavy floral sweetness.

After a few minutes more we reached the river's edge, and I was left slackjawed by what I saw on the opposite shore. It looked as if people were living in chambers that were supported somehow in the crown of an immense tree. I could see them walking about in their separate rooms, which were all framed in sprays of leaves. Then I made out gleams of what appeared to be polished walls and realized that what I'd taken for a tree must be the ruin of an ancient building, seven stories high (an estimate, because the floors were sunk down in places, elevated in others) and occupying several hundred feet of the bank, the entire structure overgrown with moss and vines, its facade crumbled away, leaving dozens of chambers open to the weather. Blankets and other types of cloth hangings were arranged over a number of these openings. Fronting the ruin was a stretch of bare rock on which several people were washing their laundry in the murky green water and then spreading it to dry. It was the Conrad Hilton of hobo jungles, and I wouldn't have been greatly surprised to see a doorman guarding the entrance, dressed in a stove-in top hat and tails, and smoking the stub of a found cigar.

There were twenty, twenty-five dogs snooting about on the rocks or just lying in the sun, and when our dogs spotted them, they all took to barking excitedly. A couple of the people waved, and I heard somebody call out to Pieczynski.

"Thought you said wasn't no people born over here," I said to Pieczynski. "So where'd that fuckin' ruin come from?"

"The hell you talkin' about?" he said. "Ain't no ruins around here."

"Then what you call that?" I pointed at the opposite bank.

He gave a snort of laughter. "That ain't no ruin, friend. That there's a tree."

About five years ago when I was riding with a female hobo name of Bubblehead, she used to read me from the children's books I carried in my pack, and there was this one had a tree in it called a monkey-puzzle tree. It had branches that would grow out sideways and then straight down; the whole thing resembled an intricate cage with all these nooks and crannies inside the branches where you could shelter from the elements. Yonder's tree might have been a giant mutant brother to the monkey-puzzle tree, but there were a few salient differences: the larger horizontal branches flattened out to form floored chambers with walls of interwoven foliage, and various of the branches that grew straight down were hollow and had been tricked out with ladders. There were ladders, too, all up and down the trunk, and elevators that worked on pulleys and could be lowered and raised between levels. I reckon there were in the high hundreds of chambers throughout. Maybe more. Only about 150 were occupied, I was told, so I had my choice. I settled myself in a smallish one close to the main trunk on the third floor; it was open on two sides, but I figured I'd find a way to close it off, and it was just the right size for me and Stupid . . . though I wasn't sure he'd be joining me. He'd run off with the other dogs as soon as he'd finished paddling across the river. The sweetish smell of the jungle was even stronger near the trunk, and I supposed it was the tree giving off that odor.

Pieczynski handed me over to a trim, tanned, thirty-something woman name of Annie Ware and went off to see to his own affairs. Annie had a sandy haircut like a boy's and wore khaki shorts and a loose blouse of stitched-together bandannas. It had been a long time since I'd looked at a woman with anything approaching a clear mind and unclouded eye, and I found myself staring at Annie. There was a calmness to her face illustrated by the fine lines around her gray eyes and mouth, and though she wasn't what you'd call a raving beauty, she was a damn sight more attractive than the women I'd encountered on the rails. She led me through the dim interior of the tree, passing several occupied chambers lit by candles, and explained how things worked in Yonder.

"We get most of our supplies from back in the world," she said. "There's five of us—Pie's one—who don't mind traveling back and forth. They scrounge what we need. Rest of us wouldn't go back for love nor money."

When I asked how come this was, she shot me a sideways glance and said, "You feel like goin' back?"

"Not right now," I told her. "But I 'spect sooner or later I'll be wantin' to."

"I don't know. You look like a stayer to me." She guided me around a corner and we came to a place where you could see out through a couple of unoccupied chambers at the jungle. The sunlight made the flattened branch shine like polished mahogany. "Everyone works here. Some people fish, some hunt for edibles in the jungle. Some weave, some cook . . ."

"I can fish," I said. "My daddy useta . . ."

"You'll be doin' chores at first. Cleaning and runnin' errands. Like that."

"Is that so?" I stopped walking and glared at her. "I been doin' for myself . . ."

She cut me off again. "We can't tolerate no lone wolfs here," she said. "We all work together or else we'd never survive. New arrivals do chores, and that's what you'll be doin' till you figure out what job suits you."

"Just who is it lays down the rules?"

"Ain't no rules. It's how things are is all."

"Well, I don't believe that," I said. "Even out on the rails, free as that life is, there's a peckin' order."

"You ain't out on the rails no more." Annie folded her arms beneath her breasts. Her eyes narrowed, and I had the impression she perceived me as an unsavory article. "Some people been here more'n twenty years. When they came, there was people here who told 'em how things worked. And there was people here even before them."

"What happened to 'em all?"

"They died . . . what do you think? Either they was killed or they just gave out. Then there's some caught a ride over Yonder's Wall."

"Them mountains, you mean?"

"Yeah, right. 'Them mountains'." She charged the words with disdain.

"You don't like me very much, do you?" I said.

Annie's mouth thinned. "Let's say I ain't disposed to like you."

"Why's that? I ain't done nothin' to you."

She twitched her head to the side as if she'd been struck and kept silent for four or five seconds. "You don't have a clue who I am, do you?" she asked finally.

I studied her for a second or two. "I never seen you before in my life."

She fixed me with a mean look. "My train name useta be Ruby Tuesday. I rode the southern line mostly, but there was times I rode up north."

"Ruby?" I peered at her, trying to see in her face—a face that radiated soundness—the wild-haired, grimy clot of human misery I'd known long years before.

"It's Annie now," she said. "I cleaned up. Same as you. Only difference is, I been living clean seven years, and you been doin' it for a day."

I couldn't believe it was her, but I couldn't disbelieve it either. Why would she lie? "What'd I do to piss you off?" I asked. "Hell, I rode with you when you's with Chester the Molester. We had some good times together."

She gaped at me, as if stunned. "You don't remember?"

"I don't know what you got in mind, but there's a whole lotta things I don't remember."

"Well, you gon' be doin' some serious rememberin' the next few weeks. Maybe it'll pop up." She spun on her heel and walked away.

"Hey, don't go!" I called after her. "I don't know where the fuck I am! How'm I gon' find my room?"

"Look for it," she snapped back. "I ain't about to stand around and hold your dick for ya!"

I did, indeed, do some serious remembering over the next week or thereabouts. Days, I fed fish heads and guts to the dogs—must have been around sixty of them all told—and carried messages and helped dig new latrines. Nights, I sat in my room, closed off from the rest of Yonder by two blankets that Pieczynski had lent me, and stared at a candle flame (candles also courtesy of Pieczynski) as the stuff of my life came bubbling up like black juice through the shell of a stepped-on bug. Not much I remembered gave me pleasure. I saw myself drinking, drugging, thieving, and betraying. And all that before I'd become a tramp. I could scarcely stand to think about it, yet that was all I thought about, and I would fall asleep each night with my head hurting from images of the bedraggled, besotted life I had led.

As the days passed I became familiar with Yonder's routine. Every morning small groups would head upriver to fish or out into the jungle to pick berries and other edibles, each accompanied by a handful of dogs. The rest took care of their work in and around the tree. On the landward side of the tree, a space had been cleared in the jungle and that's where the food preparation was done—in long pits dug beneath thatched open structures. There seemed only the loosest possible sense of community among the residents. People were civil to one another, but generally kept to themselves. At times I would wander about the tree, looking for company, and while some would say "Hi" and introduce themselves, nobody invited me to sit and chat until one night I ran into a skinny, intense kid named Bobby Forstadt, who shared a room on the fifth floor with Sharon, a blond punk girl who was decorated all over with self-applied tattoos—black words and crudely drawn flowers and the names of boys.

When Bobby found out I was new to Yonder, he invited me in and started pumping me for information about the world. I proved a major disappointment, because I hadn't paid a great deal of attention to current events the past few years. I wasn't even sure who was president, though I told him I thought it was somebody from Texas. The governor, maybe.

"Bush?" Bobby arched an eyebrow and looked at me over the top of his wire-rimmed glasses. He had a narrow, bony face that peeked out from a mass of brown curls like a fox from a hedge. "Hey, I don't think so," he said. "What about Gore?"

The name didn't set off any bells.

"Fuck! Bush?" Bobby appeared deep in thought and after a bit he said, "You musta got it wrong, man."

"I don't know," I said. "Maybe. But I was jungled up with Kid Dallas right after the election and he was shouting, 'Yee-ha!' and shit, and goin' on 'bout some Texas guy got elected."

"Bush," said Bobby, and shook his head, as if he just couldn't get his brain around the thought. He was sitting cross-legged on the floor behind a desk he'd made from a tree stump; a spiral-bound notebook was open atop it, and there were stacks of similar notebooks in one corner of the room, separated by a couple of rolled-up sleeping bags from stacks of regular books, mostly dog-eared paperbacks. One wall was dominated by a hand-drawn map constructed of several dozen taped-together sheets of notebook paper. I asked him about it, and he said it was a map of Yonder.

"It's probably not accurate," he said. "I just put together everybody's stories about how they came here and where they've traveled since, and that's what I ended up with." He cocked an eye toward me. "Where'd you catch out?"

"Klamath Falls," I told him. "Weirdest thing, 'bout maybe ten minutes out we started goin' through these mountains. Big 'uns."

"Everyone sees the same exact stuff," Bobby said. "First the mountains and the marshes. Then the hills."

"You sayin' everyone who comes to Yonder goes through the same country, no matter where they catch out?"

"Sounds fucked up, huh?" Bobby scratched at his right knee, which was poking through a hole in his jeans. He also had on a black Monster Magnet T-shirt. Circling his wrist was a bracelet woven of blond hair that I presumed to be Sharon's. "This whole place is fucked up," he went on. "I've been here going on four years, and I haven't seen anything yet that made sense."

With little prompting, he went off into a brief lecture about how various elements of the ecology of the place didn't fit together, using terms with which I was mostly unfamiliar. "When I first arrived," he said, "I thought of Yonder as Hobo Heaven, y'know. A lowball version of 'The Big Rock Candy Mountain.' Everything but the cigarette trees and the free beer. But you know what the place reminds me of now? It's like the terrain some software guy might write for a computer game. The trains and all the bizarre fauna . . . I was so freaked out when I got here, I didn't question any of it. But you examine it and you find out it's really stupid. No logic. Just this insane conglomeration of irrational objects. But it's a landscape where you could set a cool war or a puzzle game like *Myst*."

"That what you think Yonder is?" I asked. "A computer game?"

"Yeah, why not? An extremely sophisticated one. And we're the characters. The algorithms the real players inhabit." He gave a shrug that seemed to signify cluelessness. "What do you think it is?"

"Best I can come up with, I figure we're dead and this is some kinda test."

"Then how do you account for the fact that people die? And that some of us travel back to the world?"

"Never said I knew what the rules was for bein' dead," I told him. "Maybe it all fits right in."

He sat there for moment, nodded, then hopped up and went over to the stacked notebooks. "I want you to check this out," he said, digging through the stacks. "Here!" He came back to the desk and tossed me a ratty notebook with a red cover. "Read this when you get a chance, and let me know what you think."

"I can't read," I said.

He absorbed this for a two-count. "You got a disability?"

"Not that I know of. My daddy wasn't too big on school. I can sign my name, I can add and subtract. That's about it."

"You want to learn, I'll teach you."

"I reckon not. I gone this long without, it don't seem all that important now."

"I won't push it," Bobby said. "But you'd be smart to take me up on the offer. Time can move pretty slow around here."

The first grown-up book I read start to finish was a taped-together paperback entitled *Sweet Wild Pussy*. It had nothing to do with cats, nor do I believe it possessed much in the way of literary value, unless you were to count being made incredibly horny as an artistic achievement. Bobby had given it to me because the words were simple, and I felt accomplished on finishing it—the result of months of study. Still and all, I wish he had loaned me something else to begin with. Being the first thing I read, it exerted an undue influence on me for a while, and I found myself thinking overly much about "love ponies ridden hard" and "squeezable passion mounds." Eventually I got around to reading the red notebook that Bobby had pushed on me during our first meeting. It had been found on a train that had returned from Yonder's Wall and was purportedly the diary of a man named Harley Janks whom no one remembered. Harley claimed to have ridden straight from the world, past Yonder and on into the mountains. He said that beyond the mountains lay a world that was hellish hard to live in, populated by all manner of nasty critters; but there was a big settlement there and folks were carving out a place for themselves, working to bring order out of chaos. Most people who had read the notebook considered it a hoax. Harley was not a terribly articulate man, and his descriptions of life over Yonder's Wall were pretty thin. However, Bobby thought the notebook went a ways toward proving his theory that Yonder was part of a computer game, and that the world Harley described was simply the next level.

Time, as Bobby had said, did move slowly at the settlement. I came to view my life there as a kind of penance for my sins, a retreat during which I was forced to meditate upon the damage I had caused, the waste and delusion of almost my every waking hour. And maybe, I thought, that meditation was a measure of Yonder's purpose. Though the actual nature of the place continued to elude me, I realized that Bobby was right—nothing about it made sense, at least in terms of a reality that I could comprehend. I noticed all manner of peculiarities. Like for example, no one ever got pregnant, and when someone died, which happened twice during those first months, sooner or later somebody new would arrive on a train. It wasn't always a one-for-one exchange, yet from what I could tell the population had remained stable since forever. But if you strung all the peculiar things together, all you wound up with was a string of peculiar things that didn't belong together. I kept going back to what Pieczynski had said—"Why should creation be all one way?" And then I'd think how it would be for a caveman whose task it was to explain the operation of the universe judging by what he knew of the world. That was how I understood our position. We were trying to comprehend the universe from information we'd gathered while living in a humongous tree for a few months or a few years, whereas it had taken folks thousands of years to come up with the theories of creation found in some of Bobby's books. A theory, as I saw it, was a kind of net that held all the facts you knew. Back in the Stone Age, they'd only had a few basic facts and so the nets they used had been basic; but as the centuries went by and more facts came to light, the mesh of the nets necessary to contain them had grown finer and finer, and things still fell through the gaps. My feeling was they'd never come up with the perfect net, and we'd never know for sure what was going on, no matter how advanced we proclaimed ourselves to be. Maybe, I thought, first impressions were the most accurate. Maybe the old world had been created by a god, and this one was populated by the dead. It didn't make life any easier to hang your hat on those notions, but it did allow you to focus on the matter at hand.

While learning to read, I naturally spent a lot of time with Bobby. People were always stopping by his room and telling him about something they'd seen, which he would then write down in a notebook, and he introduced me to all of them. But I never struck up any friendships, and once I started reading on my own, Bobby and I stopped hanging out. Looking back, I can see that he wasn't all that interested in me—at least no more than he was interested in anyone else—and the main reason he taught me was to fill his time.

That was how things were with everyone in Yonder. You might have a friend or two, but otherwise you left everyone else to their own devices. After the first week, I hardly ever ran into Pieczynski anymore. People I'd known on the rails, and there were twelve of them, men I'd ridden with like Shaky Jake, Diamond Dave, Dogman Tony . . . they acknowledged me in passing and then went on with their oddly monastic reclaimed lives. Even Stupid kept his distance. Once every so often he'd wander up and snoot at my hand to get petted, but he had become part of the pack and spent the bulk of his day associating with his four-legged associates. For my own part, I didn't have much interest in anybody, either. It was like whatever portion of my brain was in charge of curiosity had been turned down to dim. The only constant in my life were occasional visits from Annie Ware. She never stayed long and rarely showed me anything other than a businesslike face. I guessed she was filling her time by checking up on me. I was always glad to see her. Glad all over, so to speak. But I didn't enjoy the visits much because I assumed that I had done something bad to her—I had no idea what it could have been, but I imagined the worst and felt confused and remorseful whenever she came around.

For more than six months my life was occupied by menial chores, and by studying and reading. The two favorite books I read were *Gulliver's Travels* and *Richard Halliburton's Complete Book of Marvels*, which was a travel book published a half-century before. It was full of black-and-white photographs of the pyramids and South Pacific islands and the Himalayas. When I compared them to mental snapshots of the switchyard in Topeka and tramps sleeping among piles of cow crap in a Missoula cattle pen and various hobo jungles, I wished now I'd done some real traveling back in the world instead of just riding the freights and drinking my liver stiff. Thinking what I could have seen, a world of blue sky and ice from twenty-nine thousand feet up or tropical fish swarming like live jewels in aquamarine water, it stirred me up, and I would go off exploring throughout the tree, climbing rope ladders from floor to floor, peeking into chambers where ex-hobos were engaged in mending shirts or decorating their cells, and ex-punk riders were playing chess on a makeshift board. The atmosphere reminded me of this idiot farm a Seattle judge sent me to when I was so fucked up they couldn't tell if I was sane or not, a place where you sat around all day whacked on thorazine instead of jungleberries and smeared fingerpaint all over yourself. Even though this state of affairs was preferable to the lives most of the residents had led prior to crossing the dimensional divide or the River Styx or whatever border it was that we had crossed, I just didn't understand being satisfied with it.

One morning about an hour before sunup—if it *was* a sun that rose each morning and not, as Bobby theorized, an illusion produced by the software into which our essences had been transformed—I rolled out early and waited for the fishermen and the hunting parties to set out, and when I spotted Euliss Brooks, the best fisherman in Yonder, a rickety-looking, stiff-gaited, white-bearded black man with three rods on his right shoulder, carrying a net and a bait bucket, I fell in behind him, as did a handful of dogs. He glanced at me over his shoulder, but didn't say anything and kept walking. I followed him along a path that cut inland for a mile, then angled back toward the river, rejoining it at a point where the banks widened and lifted into steep cliffs of pocked grayish black limestone, forming a cup-shaped gorge that shadowed the green water, and the perfumey heat of the jungle gave way to a profound freshness, like the smell of spring water in an old well. Birds were always circling overhead, their simple shapes like crosses against the high blue backdrop, then diving down to settle in the spiky-leaved trees that fringed the cliffs.

At the edge of the gorge was a wooden platform that could be lowered on ropes and pulleys to a ledge sixty-some feet below, just above water level—that's where Euliss did his fishing, while the dogs waited for him up top. Euliss didn't utter a word until he was ready to mount the platform, and then asked me how much I weighed.

"Hunnerd 'n fifty maybe," I said.

He mulled this over. "Reckon I'll let you go on down alone," he said. "Just hang onto the rail and don't worry it sway back and forth. Damn thing always do that."

I offered to take the bucket and the rods down with me, but he said, "Naw, you might drop 'em."

"I ain't gon' drop nothin'," I told him, annoyed—what did he take me for?

"First time down you liable to drop somethin'," said Euliss. "My word on that."

I began to lower myself, and the platform swayed sickeningly, scraping against the limestone. I gripped the rail hard. Up close, the cliff face resembled the smoke-blackened ruin of a derelict cruiser: rocky projections clumped with blue-green moss; flat surfaces hung with twists of vine; punched into here and there by caves, the largest being about five feet in diameter. As I descended past one of the cave entrances, I thought I spotted movement within. I peered into the blackness, and a wave of giddiness overwhelmed me. My vision dimmed, my throat went dry. I had a moment's panic, but that was swept aside by a rush of contentment, and then I had a sense of a shy curiosity that seemed distant from me, as if it were something brushing the edge of my thoughts, the way a cat will glide up against your leg. Allied with this was an impression of great age and infinite patience . . . and strength. A strength of mind like that you'd imagine a whale to possess, or some other ancient dweller in solitude. I lost track of myself for an unguessable time, and when I pulled myself together, I could have sworn I saw something go slithering back into the cave. Panic set in for real this time. I lowered the platform hastily, and when I jumped off onto the ledge, I shouted up at Euliss, asking him what the fuck had happened. He waved for me to send up the platform. Minutes later, after he had joined me on the ledge, I asked him again.

"Didn't nobody tell you 'bout the elders?" With effort, he bent down and plucked a large dead bug out of the bait bucket.

I half-recalled Bobby using the term, but couldn't recall exactly what he had said.

"Lookit that vine there." Euliss pointed to a long strand of vine that was hanging into the water about a dozen yards from the ledge. "Follow it on up. Y'see where it goes?"

The vine vanished into a cave mouth halfway up the cliff.

"That's one of 'em," Euliss said. "He fishin' just like us."

I studied the vine—it didn't twitch or vibrate, but I could see now that it was different from the other vines. Thicker, and a mottled gray in color.

"What are they?" I asked.

"Old hermits like to fish. Thass all I know. And I ain't crawlin' into one of them caves just to catch a look at 'em. They be fishing with that tentacle thing they got all day long." He handed me a rod —a Shimano. "Don't be mistreatin' that pole, boy. Took me most of a year to get Pie to fetch it." He straightened, heaved a sigh, and put a hand to his lower back as if to stifle a pain. "I figgered you knew 'bout the elders. Don't nobody 'cept me like fishin' here 'cause they scared of 'em. Ain't nothin' be scared 'bout. Once they touch you up, they know all they want to 'bout you, and they won't never bother you again."

The fishing itself wasn't much of a challenge. We were after the big sluggish fish with tarnished-looking scales that hid out under the rock shelves underwater; once they were hooked, they struggled briefly, then gave out and let us haul them onto the ledge. The bulk of my thoughts turned to the strange creature that had scoped me out with its tentacle, to the impression of age and patience and calm I'd derived. It occurred to me that the presence of the elders suited Bobby Forstadt's theory that we were constructs in a computer game better than it did the notion that we had passed on. They served no apparent purpose, they were window-dressing, an invention designed to appeal to twelve-year-olds—like mutant Zen monks in their shyness and simplicity, possessed of vast wisdom, bestowing calm and contentment on everyone they touched, even—I assumed —the fish they ate. Or maybe they had a hidden purpose. They might be the secret masters of this bizarre place. I was beginning to wish I'd never learned how to read. Too many ideas started rattling around in your head, and it got to where you couldn't make up your mind about anything.

"Best thing you can do," Euliss advised me, "is concentrate on fishin' and don't worry 'bout it. People 'round here worry too damn much 'bout what's goin' on. Ain't nothin' to worry 'bout. It's just God."

"God?" I said.

"That's right! You set here and fish long enough, you gon' feel Him. He's all around us—we livin' inside Him." He cocked an eye toward me. "I know you think you heard all that before, but what I'm sayin' ain't the same as you heard. You quit runnin' your mouth all the time, you'll know what I'm talkin' 'bout."

Each morning thereafter Euliss and I went out to fish; each evening we would return home and drop off our catch with the cooks. I'd thought that we might become friends, but we never did. Euliss had one topic of conversation—fishing at the gorge—and once he was done communicating whatever information he felt compelled to convey, he would fall silent until next he needed to instruct me on some point of lore. Once I asked him about his life before arriving in Yonder, and he told me he had ridden under the name of Coal Train and he been hoboing for almost fifty years. He didn't appear eager to expand on the subject, and I guess I understood that. After all the painful remembering I'd done, I had little desire to share my old life with anyone.

I woke up one day feeling poorly, and instead of going to the gorge, I slept in. Around noon, moved by restlessness, I forded the river and set off walking the path along which I had come to Yonder. Three dogs—one, the little collie that had ridden with me and Pie —fell in at my heels. I followed the path up through the jungle, then ascended the ridge line until I reached a point where I could see the tracks curling around the base of a hill. A train was standing on it, most of the cars out of sight beyond the curve. The engine and the visible cars all bore ridged scars left by beardsley attacks, and that led me to believe it was an old train. As I've said, my curiosity had been at low ebb ever since my arrival, but now I was suddenly overcome with curiosity, wondering how the trains got born and how long they lived or if those questions were even relevant. Once I had scrambled down the slope, I walked alongside the cars, examining them closely. Nowhere did I see a bolt or a seam. The entire train was of a piece—couplings and wheels and doors all seemingly grown into shape. The wheels appeared to be made of the same stuff as the cars, only thickened and harder, and the tracks they rode on weren't metal but grooved black rock that sprung from the earth. I scraped away dirt from the grade and saw that the rock was embedded to a depth of at least two feet—that was how far down I excavated. The engine had no windshield, no doors, no lights—it was just a dead black streamlined shape. How could it watch ahead? I wondered. How did it take sustenance . . . fuel? I had a hundred questions and no answers. It was like Bobby Forstadt said, nothing made any sense.

I went around the front of the engine and then walked down-train between the side of the engine and the hill. Just above the engine's rear wheel someone had spray-painted a red message, faded, but still legible:

SANTA CLAUS RODE THIS
BLACK BASTARD INTO THE EAST
HEADING OVER YONDER'S WALL

I'd never met Santa Claus, but I'd heard old hobos talk about him, much of the talk regarding what a devious piece of crap he had been, this coming from men who themselves were notable for being devious pieces of crap. They did testify that Santa Claus had been a balls-out rider, how when he was determined to catch out on a train, nothing, not the bulls, not security devices, would stop him. What interested me was why he had signed his moniker and not his birth name. Maybe, I thought, his parents had stuck him with something as unappetizing as Maurice Showalter.

I went back around to the other side of the train and sat myself down on the grade. The trains, the tree, the beardsleys, the elders, the placid, disinterested inhabitants of Yonder treading water in their lives, and Yonder's Wall—they still seemed to be pieces belonging to different puzzles. But now I wondered if Santa Claus hadn't hit on the only solution there was to all of them. What was the point in sticking around the tree and eating jungleberries and fishing and thinking about the past? Might as well see what lay beyond the mountains. Could be you'd die . . . but maybe you were already dead. For certain sure, according to everything I'd heard, you eventually were going to die from sitting on your butt. And if Bobby was right, then moving to the next level was your one chance to win.

I was going round and round with this in my head, when I spied somebody walking toward me from the curve. Soon I saw that it was Annie Ware. She had on an orange T-shirt and her khaki shorts. She looked like ice cream to the Devil. "What you doin' out here?" I asked as she came up, and she shrugged and said, "I like the trains, y'know." She stood over me for a few beats, staring off along the tracks, shifting her feet, as if feeling betwixt and between. Then, with an abrupt movement, she dropped down beside me. "Sometimes when I'm huntin' for berries, I come back this way so I can look at 'em. There's always a train waitin'."

That startled me. "Always?"

She nodded. "Yeah . . . 'least I can't recall a time when there wasn't one."

Video game, I decided. The zombies are always in the parking lot, the hamburger with the message under the bun is always served at the same café. Then I thought, Why couldn't death have that sort of predictability? All every new piece of the puzzle did was add another confusing color.

We sat without speaking for the better part of a minute, and then, for want of anything better, I said, "I know I done something to you, but I swear I can't remember it. I been tryin', too."

Her mouth thinned, but she didn't say anything.

I lifted my eyes to the sky, to the dark unidentifiable creatures that were ever circling there, gliding among scatters of cloud. "If you want me to know what I done, you probably gon' have to tell me."

A breeze ruffled the weeds alongside the grade, drifting up a flurry of whitish seed pods.

"You broke my heart, you sorry son of a bitch." Annie's eyes fixed straight ahead. "You'd been romancin' me for a long time, and finally I told you I was gonna leave Chester. We're s'posed to meet at Mother Love's in Missoula. I waited for you almost a week." She turned a steely look on me. "It was bad enough thinkin' you run out on me, but I know you fuckin' forgot! You was probably so damn stoned, you didn't even know you were hittin' on me!"

Here I'd been thinking I must have raped her, and now finding out I'd stood her up . . . well, if I'd been back in my old life that would have pissed me off good and proper. I might have laughed drunkenly and said something like, *Broke your heart? Who the fuck you think you are? A goddamn princess?* But I'd become a wiser man. "I'm real sorry," I said. "Chances are I was so messed up behind . . ."

"I realize I wasn't much back then," she went on, a quaver in her voice, "but goddammit, I think I deserved better'n to get left alone in a mission in fuckin' Missoula fightin' off a buncha ol' animals day and night for a week! I *know* I deserved better!"

"I'm sorry," I said. "I truly am. I wouldn't do it now."

"The hell's that mean?"

"Means now all the shit's been scraped off my soul, I still like you. It means that me likin' you must run deep."

She shifted like she was about to stand up, but she stayed put. "I don't . . ." she began; she drew a breath and held it for couple of seconds before letting it out. "You're just horny."

"Well, that don't mean I don't like you."

This brought a slight softening of her expression, but then she said, "Shit, I ain't listenin' to this," and got to her feet.

"C'mon, Annie. You 'member how it was back in the world." I stood up behind her. "We were fuckin' wrecks, the both of us. We'd likely have killed each other."

"That's still an option, far as I'm concerned."

It's funny sometimes how you enter into an involvement. You're not even thinking about it with the front of your mind, you're dealing with some stupid bullshit, then all of a sudden it's standing right there, and you say, Oh yeah, that's what I been wanting, that's what the back of my mind's been occupied with, and now you can't do without it. Watching the featherings of whitish blond hair beside Annie's left ear was the thing that did it for me. I put a hand on her shoulder, lightly, ready to jerk it back if she complained or took a swing at me. She flinched, but let the hand stay where it was. Then she said, "You ain't gettin' laid anytime soon, I can promise you that."

"What can I get?" I asked, trying to put a laugh in the words.

"You keep pushin', you'll find out." She stepped away, turned to me, and I could see our old trouble in her worn, still-pretty face. "Just take it slow, okay? I ain't too good at forgive and forget."

I held up my hands, surrendering.

She pinned me with another hard look, as if searching for signs of falsity. Then she gave a rueful shake of her head. "Let's go on home," she said.

"Don't you want to hang out here with the train?"

"I'm gonna hunt up some decent food and fix you dinner," she said. "I wanna find out if we can spend an evening together without makin' each other crazy." She ran her eye along the sleek curve of the engine. "This ol' train be 'long here any time I want it."

Back when I opted out of society, choosing to live free, as I perceived it then, I could have wound up on the streets in some homeless-friendly city like Portland, but I don't believe I would have made the choice I did if I hadn't loved trains. Loved their idea and their reality. Hobos were to my mind the knight templars of the homeless, carrying on a brave tradition of anti-establishment activity, like bikers and other such noble outcasts. Five years later I doubt I could have pronounced the word "anti-establishment," and the true reasons for my checking out—laziness, stubbornness, residual anger, and damn foolishness—had been wiped away by countless pints of fortified wine and enough speed to make every racehorse in America run fast. But I never lost my love for the trains, and neither had Annie.

"I 'member the first time I rode," she said. "It was the best damn feelin'! I caught me a local out of Tucson with this guy I met in Albuquerque. We found us a flatcar loaded with pipe. Right in the middle of the pipe there was this little square area that was clear. Like a nest. We got ourselves down in there and partied all the way to Denver."

This took me by surprise because it was the first time I'd heard anyone in Yonder reminisce about their life back in the world. We were sitting in Annie's room, which was half again as big as mine. Her ceiling was contrived of interwoven leaves and vines and a branch thick as a man's waist that cut across on the diagonal, and her walls were curtains made of sewn-together remnants, pieces of old skirts and sleeping bags and towels and such. She'd fashioned a mattress by stuffing a hand-sewn cover with grass—it looked a damn sight more comfortable than my old fart-sack resting on a hardwood floor. Candles fired the curtain colors with their flickering. It was a nice cozy little space.

"My first time wasn't all that great," I said. "But I know what you talkin' about."

"Tell me," she said, and this, too, surprised me. I'd grown used to people not caring about my particulars.

I drew my legs up so I was sitting cross-legged and looked down at my hands. "I was one pitiful motherfucker back then. Couldn't hold a job. Not 'cause I didn't do the work. I'd always get pissed off at somebody in authority and cuss 'em out, and that'd be that. But then I met this woman. Jesus, she was somethin'. She knew what kinda trouble she was gettin' with me, but she loved me anyway. I don't understand why to this day. She didn't try to straighten me out; she made me want to straighten myself out. But I just couldn't handle bein' happy. 'Least that's the way it seems to me now. I went to a shrink, and he told me I was always tryin' to punish myself 'cause of all the crap my daddy put me through. I told him, 'Hell, I know that. What I do about it?' And he says, 'What do you want to do about it?' I thought that was bullshit, so I got mad and walked out of his office." I picked at the cuticle on my thumbnail. "I understand now he'd seen through me. I didn't want to do anything about it. It was easier to go on bein' miserable than it was to work at bein' happy. That's what made me mad. Him knowin' that about me. I was so upset by what he'd said, I found me an ATM and took all the money out of my account. *Our* account. I was livin' with her and we'd merged our finances, such as they were. I took over seven hunnerd dollars, most of it hers. Then I went to the liquor store and bought myself a bottle of expensive whiskey. Gentleman Jack. And I headed down to the Oregon City freight yard to drink it. I wasn't plannin' on goin' nowhere, but it started to rain and I crawled into an open boxcar to finish my bottle. Next I know, train's pullin' into the switchyard at Roseville. I run into a couple hobos jungled up outside the yard. They was happy drunk, on their way to the hobo convention at Brill. Come along with us, they said. All they wanted was the crank and the booze my seven hunnerd could buy. But I figured I'd found my true companions. In a way I s'pose I had."

Saying it out loud seemed to lighten me by half, and thinking I could let go of it all just that easy, it made me wish I could unsay it, gather it back inside me. It wasn't something I felt I should ever be free of, even for a few seconds.

"What was her name?" Annie asked.

"Eileen," I said.

The name lay like a puddle that had formed between us, but when Annie spoke again, it seemed to evaporate.

"Damn near everyone here got a past needs livin' down," she said. "Only option we got is to make the best of what is."

"That don't hardly seem like enough."

We sat for a while without speaking. It started to rain—I could hear it coming down heavy through the curtains, but we were so deep inside the tree, none of the drops penetrated the canopy. It felt like we were in a bubble of light submerged in a rushing river.

"Somethin' else I better tell you," I said. "I been thinkin' 'bout catchin' out again."

Her face appeared to sharpen, but she remained silent.

"Maybe headin' out east," I said. "Takin' a trip through the mountains."

"That's crazy," she said quietly. "Don't nobody come back from there."

"You sayin' you never thought about it? I don't believe that. I know why you hangin' 'round the trains."

"Sure, I thought about it." Annie's voice was hard the way your voice becomes when you're suppressing emotion. "Life here . . . It ain't livin', it's just bein'. There's times I considered takin' that trip. But that ain't what I call it."

"What do you call it?" I asked.

"Checkin' out," she said.

"Maybe there's somethin' there."

"Yeah, right!"

"Seriously," I said. "What's the point of all this bullshit if there ain't somethin' out there?"

Annie gave a sarcastic laugh. "Oh, I see. There's gotta be a point. Worst thing about this place is havin' to listen to a buncha tramps settin' 'round philosophizin'!" She affected a crotchety voice. "Yonder's the borderland between life and death. It's a computer game, it's new world a'buildin'. It's a little scrap of reality left over from creation, like the scraps get left over from a cookie cutter."

"I never run across that last 'un," I said.

Annie snorted in disgust. "Stick around! You'll hear crazier'n that. I realize most people here just got their brains back, but ain't none of 'em geniuses. They'd be better off tryin' to figger out what to do 'bout the fritters, or somethin' practical, 'steada studyin' on what's to come and why."

"Tell me 'bout the fritters," I said. "Nobody ever wants to talk about 'em. They just say they're dangerous."

"I don't really know what they are. They look like apple fritters and they float around in the air. They got some kinda poison'll kill you quick."

I gave a chuckle. "Must be all that deep fat fryin' it takes to make 'em."

"You think they're funny?" Annie soured on the conversation. "Now the rains come, won't be long 'fore you find out exactly how funny they are."

I had to admit Annie was right—listening to a bunch of hobos philosophize, the majority of them with less than high school educations, wasn't all that entertaining. But philosophizing was a natural outgrowth of life over Yonder. Most people spent six or seven hours a day working, and most had a relationship of some type that served to pass the time; but there was usually idle time, and even though everybody's curiosity—like my own—seemed to have been diminished, the question of where-the-hell-are-we was bound to pop up whenever you let your thoughts drift. Talk to a person more than once, and they'd tell you how they stood on the matter. My informal poll showed that about a third of the residents believed we had passed over into some borderland of death and were being tested to determine where we would end up. Maybe a quarter believed that railroad yards back in the world were areas where the borders between dimensions blurred, and that we had switched tracks, so to speak, and no test was involved. About twenty percent adhered to Bobby's computer game theory, but I think this number was skewed because Bobby was evangelical about the theory and had influenced a sizable portion of the punk riders to buy into it. The rest of the people had more individualized theories, although they generally played off one of the three main ideas.

One of the strangest and certainly the most explicit of these theories came to me from Josiah Tobin, a fiftyish man who still had the nasty-looking gray Moses beard he'd worn when he'd been a hobo known as Froot Loop, and was a member of the FTRA (Freight Train Riders of America), a group of tramps, a gang of sorts, who'd thought of themselves as big time macho badasses, but were mainly dead-on-their-feet drunks. The irony of this was that Froot Loop was gay. The FTRA would never have initiated him if they'd been aware of his homosexuality. Once they found out, they chose to ignore the fact rather than beat the crap out of him and drum him from the ranks, which establishes to my mind how badass they actually were. Anyway, I was doing my laundry one afternoon, letting my clothes dry and sunning myself, lying shirtless with my hands behind my head, watching the clouds, while Josiah was doing the same. He'd pushed his beard aside to expose his scrawny chest, and the untanned portion resembled a permanent pale bib. We fell to conversing about this and that, and eventually he told me what he thought had happened to us.

"Way I figger," he said, "there's more universes than they got zeros to count 'em. Trillions and trillions of 'em, and they all 'bout a hair apart, so it's easy to slip over into the ones is close to your own.

I'm talkin' *real* easy. Like you know how it is when you lose your keys or somethin'—you know just a second ago you set 'em down on the coffee table, but they ain't there. Well, you ain't wrong. That's where you did set 'em. What happened is you slipped over into a universe where you set 'em somewheres else. Hell, you might stay there the rest of your life. You with me so far?"

"Oh, yeah," I said. "Keep it comin'."

"Now the universes close by," Josiah went on, "they're a whole lot like the one you in. Might just be one or two things differnt, like where you put your keys or what time your favorite show comes on the TV. But the farther away the universes get from your universe, the weirder they are. One a billion universes away, it might be so differnt you wouldn't be able to understan' nothing what's goin' on. Still hangin' in there?"

"Yep," I said.

"Okay. Every once in a while there's a crack opens. I ain't talkin' 'bout a crack 'tween universes. I'm talkin' 'bout a crack in the whole damn structure. Things fall through them cracks, where you think they go?"

"Yonder," I said.

"Or someplace like Yonder. I figger there's bound to be more'n one of 'em. How them places start up . . . I don't know. I'm studyin' on it, though." Josiah lifted his head to look at me. "Whatcha think?"

"I like it. Makes more sense than Bobby Forstadt's theory."

Josiah snorted. "That computer game horseshit! All that goes to show is how Bobby spent his time back in the world."

"One thing I don't get," I said, "is the trains. They don't seem to fit nobody's theory. And the way you feel after the first night. Healthy and clear-headed. That sure seems like stuff I been told happens when you die."

"The folks that told you all that stuff hadn't died, had they? It's just as likely it'll purify a man to cross over the border between universes. But the trains . . . I hate to say you're right, but you're right. I come up with a few explanations that fit my theory. They're pretty goddamned harebrained, but I'm workin' on somethin' better."

He turned onto his stomach. His back was striped with thickly ridged scars, some of the tissue twisted up into knots—I'd seen similar scars on a tramp who'd had a run-in with some barbed wire.

"I'll figger somethin' out," Josiah said. "Somethin'll come along to fit in there sooner or later."

*   *   *

Josiah had a lot more confidence that there was going to be a "later" than most. As the rains heavied, lasting longer every day, people grew anxious and kept to their rooms. Annie and I, too, stayed at home more than we once had, but not because of anxiety. We had moved past the getting-to-know-you stage and spent lazy mornings on her grass mattress, listening to raindrops smacking like soft bullets into the canopy, talking and doing what I once would have referred to as "fucking," but now, as I recognized the mutuality of the act and wasn't just trying to satisfy myself, I thought of as making love.

We came to talk about the past more often than not—the present just wasn't that interesting. Annie told me she had run a successful cleaning business in Tucson, and it was stress related to the business that had driven her out of society and onto the rails. One morning, she said, she woke up and simply couldn't handle the pressure anymore. Though when I'd known her before, she'd been almost as dissolute as me, she held a more romantic view of the life than I did. She recalled it as being a party with friends that had lasted for years, and the terrible things that had happened to her —rape and beatings and such—had been anomalies. She was glad to be away from that life, but she had good memories that superseded all the bad; she would go on about the freedom, the parties, the hobo conventions, the fellowship. Often she talked about how she had gotten married to Chester the Molester in the yard at Spokane, how tramps had come from everywhere, and a couple of trampettes had worked a job in Klamath Falls for nearly a month so they could buy her a ring. I believe it was this romantic side that had caused her to fall for me. She'd contrived an image of me as being a real King of the Road and not the falling-down drunk that I truly was; despite me standing her up in Missoula, she had clung to that image, nourished it like an article of faith. For my part, I was so thankful to be with anyone, at first I couldn't separate those feelings out from what I felt for her. But with the passage of days, I came to realize I loved everything about her. The way the muscles in her calves bunched when she walked, the expressiveness of her smiles, the variety of her moods. How she'd stare at a piece of cloth that Pie or somebody had brought back from the world until she recognized the shape in it, and the next you know it would be a shirt or a skirt or a pair of trousers. The thing I loved most about Annie was her strength. Not that she was entirely strong. We each had a crack down through the middle of us, the same that had disabled our old lives. Nevertheless she had a strength about her, one built on endurance and tolerance that seemed partner to the strength I had started to see in myself. Maybe that fit was what allowed us to love one another.

One morning we were lying in late, being easy together, when the dogs set up a baying, as they sometimes would, only this was louder and more prolonged than usual. Annie sat up in bed, the sheet falling away from her breasts, and listened. I made a grab for her, but she pushed my hand away and said, "Quiet!" Within a matter of seconds, the barking diminished, but didn't stop altogether. Soon I heard solitary barks closer at hand, and then the clitter of paws as dogs went running past our room.

"They're here," Annie said in a dead voice.

"What?" I sat up beside her and looked at her despairing face. She didn't answer, and I said, "You mean the fritters?"

She nodded.

I jumped up from the bed. "Let's go! Let's get outa here!"

"Don't do no good," she said, hanging her head.

"The hell you mean?"

"It don't do no good," she said sternly, almost angrily. "Ain't nowhere to go. Safest place we can be is right here."

A dog, a black Lab mix like Stupid, only bigger, poked his head in through the curtained doorway, woofed, and then retreated.

"The dogs can protect us here," Annie said. "There's not a damn thing else we can do 'cept set right where we are."

"That's crazy! We can fight 'em."

"You can't fight 'em. Try and hit 'em with a stick, a machete, they just slip away. It's like they know it's comin'. And if they touch you, you're a goner."

I couldn't accept this. "There's gotta be somethin' we can do!"

"Come back to bed, Billy," she said, giving me a steady look. "If there was anything to do, don'tcha think I'd be doin' it?"

I ducked back under the covers and we lay there most of the day, listening to dogs snarling and barking, to distant screams, and to some less distant that caused me to squeeze Annie so hard I was worried afterward that I had hurt her. We comforted each other, said things were going to work out all right, but I could tell Annie didn't buy it, so I couldn't believe it myself. Being afraid is an awful thing, but being helpless and afraid is like being buried alive. I felt I was suffocating, every second stretching out and wrapping me in a freezing fist, with my heart sounding huge and thudding in my ears. Even after darkness fell and Annie told me that the fritters weren't aggressive at night, I couldn't completely escape that feeling. I had to do something, and when Annie fell asleep I sneaked out of the room and went to see what was up. Dogs were roaming throughout the tree, their eyes glowing yellow in the dimness, and other people were having a look-see, holding up lanterns, speaking in soft bewildered voices. I ran into Pie. The lines in his homely face appeared to have sunk deeper, and he had nothing good to tell me.

"Nearly thirty's dead," he said. "Josiah Tobin and Bo Myers. Nancy Savarese. They ain't never come at us this bad. Must be thousands of 'em this year."

"You saw 'em?" I asked.

"Naw, not all of 'em." He rubbed his chin. "I seen 'em coming for Yonder once couple years after I crossed. I don't need to see it again."

But I needed to see it. I followed the weave of limbs up high in the tree until I was forced to climb, not walk, and found a spot where I could sit astraddle of one of the branches close to the edge of the canopy, and there I waited until first light. Then I eased forward so I could see out between the leaves. They did resemble fritters. Pale brown and round and lumpy, sort of like misshapen dinner plates, thick through the middle of the body, with thin rippling edges. All floating above the river between the walls of vegetation. Pie had been right in his estimate. There must have been thousands of them. Singly, they didn't seem much of a threat, but glimpsed altogether, drifting aimlessly, many in sharp silhouette against the gray sky—they had the look of an impossible armada, an invasion of pale brown jellyfish, utterly evil and strange. I say they were drifting aimlessly, but as I watched they began a general movement toward the tree as if borne on the breeze; yet there was no breeze I could feel, and I realized they were launching a leisurely attack, gradually closing the distance between themselves and the edge of the canopy. I scrambled back along the branch and began my descent, hurrying along, less fearing a misstep than seeing a wave of fritters pushing their way through the leaves. On reaching the lower branches, I began to run, becoming lost at one point and having to retrace my steps. I was cotton-mouthed, and my pulse raced. I imagined myself surrounded by stinging, burning, flimsy scraps of death. At length I came to a populated level, saw curtains hanging over doors, and believed I was safe. I stood a moment to calm my heart. Dogs were barking down below, but I heard nothing near to hand. I set out again, passing along a stretch of limb that was tightly enclosed by walls of leaves so thick, no light could penetrate. As I came to a bend, a dog snarled up ahead of me, a violent engine of a sound that made my breath catch.

With a cautious step, I rounded the bend. I should, I suppose, have backed away, but things would doubtless have gone the same had I done so. Stupid was standing between me and two fritters floating head-high in the passage, trembling as if responding to some impalpable current. I spoke his name. His tail wagged, but his ears were laid flat, and before I could speak again, he leaped twisting in the air and snagged one of the fritters by its edge, dragged it down and began worrying it, holding it between his paws and tearing. The thing emitted a faint squeal, like air leaking from a balloon, and as Stupid continued to kill it, the second fritter slid downward, edge first, like a falling Frisbee, and plastered itself to the side of his head. Stupid yelped, rolled onto his side, trying to pry the thing loose, and succeeded in dislodging it; but it settled on him once again, on his flank. He struggled to his feet, snapping at it, his body bent almost double. Annie had told me that dogs were less sensitive to the fritters than people—they could withstand quite a bit of poison, whereas a touch would kill a man. But apparently Stupid had absorbed close to his limit. When the fritter lifted from him, he staggered to the side, his lips drawn up in a silent snarl, wobbled, then toppled off the limb and down through the leaves without a sound. I had no time to grieve, for I found myself confronting the fritter that had killed him. It was not, as I'd thought, a uniform color, but mottled with whitish patches, and it had the aspect not of an entire creature, but instead seemed a piece of one, a slimy organ that might have been removed from the body of some diseased monstrosity. Its edges rippled, the way the edges of a crepe will ripple from the heat of the griddle beneath, and I took the trembling it displayed for agitation. Full of dread, I eased a pace backward, and then, recognizing I was done for any way it shook out, not wanting it to touch me, I jumped through the leafy wall on my left and fell.

If I had jumped to my right, the direction in which Stupid had vanished, I would have fallen to my death. But instinct or luck directed me the opposite way, and I fell only about ten feet, crashing through the leafy ceiling of the room belonging to an elderly hobo with hair and beard gone almost totally white, whom I knew as SLC, which stood for Salt Lake City, his home—I hadn't spoken to him since my arrival and had not bothered to learn his real name. I landed half on his mattress, my head bonking on the floor, but though I took a pretty good whack, I didn't lose consciousness. SLC was sitting on some pillows in the corner of the room, calm as you please, eating a bowl of soup. When I managed to shake off the dizziness and sat up, he said, "Thanks for dropping in," and chuckled.

I noticed he was wearing a threadbare gray suit, a dingy white shirt, and a wide silk foulard tie of a style that I'd only seen in old black-and-white movies. He saw me registering this, apparently, because he said, "Thought I'd put on my buryin' suit . . . just in case. Them fritters gonna get me, I'll be prepared." He peered at me and blinked rapidly. "Reckon they almost got you. Was there a bunch of 'em?"

"Just one." My head started throbbing. I thought about Stupid and all the bad good times we'd shared, and felt sadness wadding up in my chest. I glanced at the hole I'd put in SLC's ceiling, expecting to see the fritter that had killed Stupid and maybe some of his pals. Nothing but leaves and shadow.

"Might as well get comfortable," SLC said. "Gonna be a long day." In his shabby finery, with stiffened hanks of white hair hanging to his shoulders, his food-stained beard, and his bony wrists and ankles, he looked like an elf gone to seed.

"I ain't stayin' here," I told him, and made to stand; but the effort got me dizzy again.

"Wouldn't be surprised you had yourself a concussion," SLC said. He slurped up another spoonful of soup. "I took a knock on the head once left me confused for a week."

"I'll be all right in a minute," I said.

I had a look around SLC's room. Taped to one wall, almost entirely covering it, were dozens of dog-eared and faded Polaroids, most photographs of natural scenery. Probably places he'd traveled. There were a few books and magazines scattered on the floor beside his mattress. Some clothes neatly piled. Two old pipe tobacco tins that likely contained sewing materials and such. Tins of Sterno and a stack of canned tomato soup. The whole place smelled like ripe hobo.

Taking stock of SLC's meager possessions steadied me, and I gave standing another try, but I was still too dizzy. I was scared and pissed off—I wanted to get back to Annie—and I said, "I don't know why the fuck you just sittin' round waitin' to die, man."

"That's all I'd be doin' things was normal," said SLC. "Sit or stand, don't make much difference."

"What I can't figure is, how come people don't move outa the way of these things."

"Where you suggest we move to? Ain't nothin' out there 'cept more jungle, and can't live on the plain 'cause the beardsleys is all over."

"Have you looked?" I asked. "You hunted around for a better place?"

"Much as I'm goin' to look." SLC set down his soup, sucked on his teeth. "You wanta look, you go on ahead."

"Maybe I will." I heaved myself up and this time I managed to make it to my feet.

"Well, that's fine. But I recommend you stay where you are for now. Goin' out in the passageways is a damn sight more dangerous."

The room did a half spin, and I leaned against the wall.

"Got yourself a concussion . . . oh yeah!" SLC said brightly. "Best thing for you is to sit on back down. I'll heat you some soup."

In my dazed condition, the prospect of sitting down for a bowl of hot soup was appealing for the moment, but the next minute, the thought of slurping tomato soup while thousands of poisonous pancakes fluttered about killing dogs and people seemed like the peak of insanity. Still unsteady, I started for the door.

"Hang on, boy!" SLC set his bowl on the floor and stood—it took him a couple of tries before he made it upright. "If you ain't got sense enough to stay put, I best go with you. Way you're staggerin', you ain't gon' get very far by yourself."

I'm not sure what was on SLC's mind. He might have been so senile, he'd forgotten the reason he had for keeping to his room. Or maybe he was so old, he figured he wasn't risking all that much. He latched onto my elbow and we started off. We passed a couple of bodies, their faces branded with empurpled blazes where they had been touched by fritters, but luck was with us and we didn't meet up with any ourselves. Once I thought I saw some floating off from us a ways on a branch two levels down, but I was seeing lots of floating things and I couldn't be sure if any of them were real. As for SLC, he hobbled along, muttering to himself, acting no different than he usually did, except every so often he would glance up at me and flash a snaggletoothed grin.

When we pushed through the curtained door into Annie's room, I thought she was going to throw us back out. She yelled at me, said how she thought I was dead, and what was I . . . Crazy? Didn't I know any better than to go sniffing around after something that would kill me? She cried, she yelled some more, called me names. Finally I put my arm around her, agreed with everything she said for about ten or fifteen minutes, and she calmed down enough to sit with me on the mattress.

"I thought you was dead," she said. "You didn't come back, and I just knew they'd got you."

"I shouldn't have gone," I told her. "It was dumb."

"It was way more'n dumb! It was . . ." She couldn't find the words and so I chimed in, saying, "It was irresponsible."

"You make it sound like you was late for work or somethin'. You coulda been killed." She looked gloomily down at my hand, which was resting on the blanket next to hers, as if she saw in it a bad sign she'd not noticed before. "I thought you'd changed."

"Hey!" said SLC. He had settled in the corner and was sitting with his knees drawn up, looking worried. "Ain't y'all got anything to eat in here?"

In the morning the fritters were gone. They took sixty-three souls with them, about a quarter of Yonder's population. We burned the bodies on the stones where usually the laundry was stretched to dry, and scattered the ashes in the river. I went to Josiah Tobin's wake, which consisted of eight old hobos sitting in his room, chewing jungleberries, and reminiscing about Josiah, telling lies about what a great rider he was and how he'd foxed the bulls in Yakima that one time, and didn't he fry up the best hobo hash you'd ever tried? I felt like a young heathen among them. I wanted to say that stories about how Josiah had pissed his life away didn't tell nothing of the man, and that to my mind he was the smartest son of a bitch I'd ever met on the rails, and the thing we should study on was not the mess he'd made of himself, but what he could have been if he'd given life more than half-a-try. But when it came my turn to speak, I told a story about drinking out in a desert squat east of Phoenix with him and Ragbone Sally. I guess I figured saying what I had thought wouldn't mean much to anyone except Josiah.

Once the funerals were done, life over Yonder went back to normal. It was like nothing had happened. I tried to resist the impulse to embrace the sense of relief that caused us to want to put the attack behind us, but I didn't try hard enough—a few days later I started going fishing with Euliss Brooks again, and me and Annie got back on track, and the tree where we all lived regained its customary lethargic atmosphere. My jungleberry consumption increased for a while, and Bobby Forstadt was, for about the same length of time, a bit more strident about his computer game theory, saying that the recurring menace of the fritters fit right in, and what we should be doing was attempting to influence the game. That was a fair sample of our reaction to sixty-three deaths. It wasn't natural, but I suppose I'd become a full-on citizen of Yonder, and the unnatural responses of my fellows no longer struck me as being out of line. But I wasn't happy. Annie and I were growing closer, but there was nowhere to go with it. If we had been back in the world, maybe we would have gotten off the rails and found regular work and built some sort of a life together; but what could you build living in a tree like kids on a backyard camp-out. We talked about catching out without any goal other than the filling up of time. We talked about returning to the world and giving it a go, but our talk was energyless and never got too serious.

Some people in Yonder kept calendars, recorded the passage of days, but I didn't catch the habit—the days generally were so much alike, they seemed one long day striped with nights, and I saw no point in marking them. Thus I'm forced to estimate that it was about three weeks after the fritter attack when things turned for me. I was out fishing with Euliss, and at midmorning we decided that since we hadn't had much success sitting together in the middle of the stone ledge, we'd try our luck at opposite ends of the ledge. It had rained overnight, and the sun was out, putting dazzles on the eddies, and the fishing should have been good, but neither one of us had gotten a nibble. The only odd thing I noticed was that the elders had reeled in their tentacles. When I mentioned this to Euliss, asked if he'd ever seen anything like it, he said maybe there was a day when it had happened before, but he wasn't sure. Then he advised me to concentrate on my fishing and pushed the brim of his baseball cap down over his eyes, signaling that he wasn't inter-ested in talking. We were sitting about thirty feet apart, and I was watching the flow of the green water about my line when out of the corner of my eye I glimpsed a rippling out at the center of the gorge. I was about to call it to Euliss's attention, but he beat me to the punch and shouted, "Got me somepin'!"

I clambered to my feet, dusted the seat of my trousers. "Is it a big 'un?" I asked, thinking I'd walk over and see what he'd hooked.

"I can't feel it now," he said. "It's waitin' on me. But yeah, it's pretty big."

I rubbed at a ground-in patch of limestone dust on my knee, and just as I glanced up, the water seemed to lift directly in front of Euliss, to bell upward, and something huge leaped half its body out from beneath the surface. A fish. It resembled a giant bass more than anything, but its scales were mud-brown, barely distinguish-able from one another, and set in its mouth were double rows of triangular teeth the color of old ivory. It twisted in its leap, angling its massive ancient-looking head toward Euliss, and as it fell, its mouth—which was the size of a garage door—came down over Euliss and snapped, biting him with such force that it took the old man's upper half and left the lower sitting there on the ledge, wobbling and spurting blood.

I've had to put together the detail I've related in retrospect, because at the moment it happened I was too stunned to do more than record the event. It just seemed that some vast darkness had sounded from the depths and severed Euliss's body, then vanished with a splash that went forty feet high. The old man's lower half sat for a second or two, rocking slightly. Despite the blood staining his britches and the rock beside him, the sight seemed unreal, a cartoon. Then it toppled into the churning water. I fell back against the wall of the gorge and pissed myself. I think I may have screamed. I pushed hard against the wall, wanting to disappear into the rock behind me, certain the thing was going to leap up again and have me for its second course. I couldn't muster a thought, I was all fear and trembling, no more mindful than a bird hypnotized by a serpent, empty of life already, knowing I belonged to death now. What broke me from my freeze was a dry slithering sound from above. I looked up and saw the nearest elder was letting down its tentacle, ready for some fishing now the danger had gone. All the rest of the elders were doing the same. The water flowed green and unperturbed.

I wasn't sure I could walk, but I managed to cross to the elevator and pull myself up to the top of the gorge. There I sat down and shivered, holding my drawn-up knees. Whatever the chemicals are that combine to make fear, they must trigger a hellacious amount of heat, because I had never felt so cold. As the cold subsided, I told myself I should get back to Annie. I wanted to touch her, to be sure of her, of something. But I wasn't ready to take that long walk alone. I stared at the water. Smooth as a jade floor. I imagined Euliss's blood threading into pink rills beneath it, and that got me moving. All the way back to the tree, my head was full of a dark shape that didn't separate out into thoughts until I was almost at Annie's door.

When I entered she glanced up from her sewing, and said happily, "You're back early? You catch all y'need?"

I sat cross-legged on the mattress facing her, leaned forward and rested my head on her shoulder. She stroked my hair, and the warmth of her hand pointed up the cold that was still inside me. I wrapped her in my arms, and she said, "What's that smell?" She touched my thigh, drew back her fingers. "You pissed your pants! Get off my bed!"

"Euliss is dead," I said.

"What?" She peered at me. "What happened?"

As I told her, as I described the event, what I wanted to do became clearer and clearer, until finally it was solid in me, the rightness of its shape discernible, like a ruby in a glass of water. "I'm going over the Wall," I said. "Today."

Annie had been listening with her head down; she looked at me now in her steady way and said, "It's a horrible thing . . . Euliss. But you're overreacting."

"Come with me," I said.

She shook her head. "I can't."

"Annie . . . for God's sake! We can't just sit here and wait to die."

"What else is there to do? It was the same back in the world. And if there's a world other side of the Wall, it'll be the same there. It's what folks do."

"That's true," I said. "But it don't make it right."

A couple of people passed by outside, talking, and for no good reason, as if we had a secret to keep, we remained silent until the voices receded.

"I'm going," I said. "I want you to go with me."

She wouldn't look at me.

"Goddamn it!" I smacked the mattress with my fist. "If you were back home, living in a country that lost twenty-five percent of its population, you'd do more than just sit."

"The hell I would! I'd stay right where I was, and I'd try to build up what was knocked down. It's what any reasonable person would do."

"All right," I said. "But this ain't the world. Every year the fritters come . . . and things like whatever it was took Euliss. Every year you got 'bout a one-in-four chance of dying."

"So you're gonna leave me?"

"I asked you to come along. You stay, it's you leavin' me."

"You ain't changed a bit!" she said. "You're still . . ."

"Yes, I have! We both of us changed. And we don't have to act like the people we used to be. Like a coupla fucked-up drunks can't agree what kinda wine to kill themselves with." I put my hands on her shoulders. "You know I'm right about this, Annie. You're all the time hangin' out there with the trains 'cause you know what I know. It's death to stay here." I thought of Josiah Tobin. "And it'll come sooner than later."

She refused to budge, and I said, "Anybody ever seen a fish like the one ate Euliss?"

Sullenly, she said, "Way you describe it, how can I tell?"

"A big brown fuckin' bass with big yellow teeth," I said. "It looked like a picture out of a children's book more'n a real fish. Like the kind of monster a child might make up. That's plain enough."

"I don't think so," she said. " 'Least I can't remember if anyone ever said anything to me about it."

"See what's happenin'? This place keeps comin' up with new ways to kill you. It's gonna get worse."

"I don't care what you say, I'm not leavin'!"

A silence wedged between us.

"Well, I guess that's it then," I said.

"I guess so." After a couple of ticks, she said, "I don't want you to go."

I was tired of arguing, but I couldn't think of a response.

"Maybe if you wait a while," she said. "We got a year 'fore the fritters come again. Maybe if you let me build up to it . . ."

"I could do that. A couple hours ago, I was sittin' with Euliss with our lines in green water, and then somethin' tore up from hell and took him. It don't seem anybody could change my mind on leavin' after seein' that, but bein' here with you now, all the comfort you are, I believe I could fall back into the way it was. But that doesn't mean it's what I should do." I tapped my head. "This here's tellin' me to leave. I never listened to my brain before, I always went with my heart, and all that did was bury me in deeper shit."

"Oh, I see! That's what I am. Deeper shit!"

"I ain't gonna argue. You know that's not what I mean. You gotta listen to your brain, too. You do, and we'll be catchin' out of this goddamn place in a hour."

She stared at me for a second, then lay down on her side, facing toward the leafy wall.

"Annie?"

"Just go," she said in a small voice.

I dropped down beside her, but she said, "Don't! I want you to go if you're goin'."

I made to warm her up by rubbing her shoulder. She snapped at me and curled into a fetal position. It felt as if a hundred pounds of wet cement had been poured into my skull, but that wasn't nearly enough to extinguish the bright point of certainty that was urging me to leave. I got up from the bed and started stuffing clothes into my pack. Several times I stopped packing and tried again to convince Annie to join me, but she wasn't hearing me. My movements grew slower—I didn't want to abandon her. But I kept at it until my goods were all tucked away. I shouldered the pack and stood looking down at her.

"This how you want to do it?" I asked.

"It's how you want it. I'm just lyin' here."

I waited a few seconds, thinking she might relent. Finally I said, "I love you, Annie."

The words caused her to flinch, but she kept silent.

It was a lot harder leaving Annie than it had been to leave Eileen —I had no whiskey to ease my path. Tears cut down my cheeks, and I must have decided a dozen times to turn back. But something kept me going and I climbed down from the tree and walked out onto the stony section of the bank and stood scanning the wall of jungle on the far side of the river. Bobby Forstadt and his punky blond girlfriend were sitting cross-legged on the rocks. They shaded their eyes against the sun, which had broken through the overcast, and stared at me.

"Where you goin'?" Bobby asked.

"East," I said. I didn't feel like talking to him, but I knew I'd have to.

"No shit!" He scrambled up to his feet. "How come?"

"Bobby, I don't feel much like talkin', all right. Go talk to Annie and she'll tell you. She's up in her room."

"Naw, she ain't." His girlfriend pointed back toward the tree. "She's right there."

Annie was coming out from under the shadow of the tree, dragging her pack along the ground—she must have stuffed it in record time. She was wearing faded jeans and an old sweatshirt. I grinned at her, but as she approached she dialed down my pleasure by saying, "You better be right about this, you son of a bitch."

Bobby cupped his hands and shouted, "Annie and Billy Long Gone . . . catchin' out over the Wall!" Then he repeated it, except instead of "catchin' out over the Wall" he said, ". . . movin' to the next level." People filtered out of the jungle, dropped from the tree, and before long we had a crowd of maybe twenty, twenty-five gathered around, asking why we were leaving and what they could do. Annie stood mute, and I fielded the questions as best I could. The news about Euliss sobered the mood, but even so nobody appeared to grasp why we were leaving. Except maybe for Pie. He shouldered his way to me and handed me a packet of dried fish wrapped in leaves and a can of red spray paint.

"I kinda figgered I'd be the one going over the Wall," he said. "But I guess it ain't in me. Hope you make it, Billy. When you get where you goin', paint me a message on the train."

"I'll do'er," I said, and we shook on it.

More people came, bringing so much food, we couldn't have carried half of it. Annie got to hugging her friends, and some folks started singing, and everybody was sharing food, and I could see it was turning into a party and was afraid if we stayed much longer we'd get caught up in it. I shouted "Hey!" and kept shouting it until I had everyone's attention. Then I said, "Thank y'all for comin' down to see us off! We appreciate it! But we're gon' be leavin' now!"

"What's the hurry?" somebody shouted, and several people laughed.

"I tell you what the hurry is," I said. "This place kills somethin' in us. It makes us settle for half a life. Maybe one reason we settle for it is that's more'n most of us ever had. But there's somethin' else goin' on, though I couldn't put a name on it. Somethin' that makes us just set around waitin' to die. It'd be easy for me'n Annie to hang out and party. Hell, after a good party, we might change our minds. But I ain't gon' let that happen."

Some people broke off from the edge of the crowd and walked away.

"This ain't nothin' to celebrate," I went on. "We ain't happy to be leavin'. We're rollin' the dice. But this way we get to do the rollin' ourselves. Staying here's the same as not even pickin' 'em up. And all that gets you is what you already know. What Euliss Brooks knew. What Josiah Tobin and Nancy Savarese knew. And the rest of 'em who ain't here to party, what they knew. We're leavin' 'cause it's our only chance of breakin' through to somethin' better. Yonder ain't no place to build a life. It's a place where you get your shit together 'fore you move on again. It's a goddamn homeless shelter with a view. We ain't s'posed to live here, we're s'posed to stop over for a while and then be gone. That's why we're leavin'. We want to find us a home."

More of the crowd had drifted away as I spoke—it appeared there were no more than ten people left. Pie, Bobby Forstadt and his girlfriend, and some others.

I adjusted the weight of my pack and said, "Thanks for the send-off. Maybe we'll see you down the road." Then I picked my way down the bank and set out to ford the river. I didn't look back, but I heard Anne splashing after me and somebody called out, "Safe rails!" By the time we reached the other side of the river, everybody except Bobby Forstadt and his girlfriend had gone, and they were back to sitting as they'd been before they saw me, talking and gesturing—Annie and I already a closed entry in Bobby's notebooks. To tell the truth, I felt the same way about Yonder. The people I'd met there had been turned into memories, and in my mind I was already going over the Wall. The tree, with its multileveled canopies and chambers, its dark gleaming branches, once again had the look of a ruin, and I supposed that was all it had truly ever been.

I half-expected the jungle to try and thwart our departure, to send legions of bugs and snakes and whatever else it could muster against us; but we reached the tracks without incident. A black train was waiting, bending around the curve of the green hill. A young one, unscarred and gleaming. I'd been hoping for the train Santa Claus had ridden—at least I knew that one could make the trip. We crawled into one of the cars and settled in, and less than five minutes later we started to roll.

I wish I had thunder and lightning in my words to tell you of that trip, because it deserves to be written large and luminous and noisy; but the world doesn't sing that song through me, and I'm stuck with speaking in a plainer voice. It began ordinarily enough. Annie was still angry at me for forcing her hand, but she was more scared than angry, and she sat with her knees drawn up, picking at frays in the knees of her jeans. I watched the hills passing out the door of the car, thinking maybe I shouldn't have pulled Annie into this, that it might have been kinder just to go without a word. I was glad to be on the move once again. It may be that the universe has no rhyme or reason, but I couldn't accept that a bunch of hobos had been brought to Yonder merely because they fell down the same crack, and so while I was scared, too, I was excited in a way I'd never been before. I wasn't just looking for a new place to take a leak in, a new town where I could run hustles and sell emergency food stamps for crank; I had a sense of myself as an adventurer, an explorer, a penetrator of the unknown. Maybe this notion was bogus, overblown, but it had been a long time since I had perceived myself in such a clean light, and I wasn't about to spoil the feeling this gave me by overanalyzing the situation.

I tried talking to Annie, but she wasn't up for it. However, after we'd gone about a mile, she scooted over and tucked herself under my arm, and we sat like that for the better part of an hour, until the train started winding down out of the hills. Through cuts between the hills we could see that yellowy green plain laid out under a high sun, and the blue dazzles of the lakes scattered across it. The windy rush of the train and the brilliant light made it all seem hopeful, as did the rich decaying smell of the marshlands as we swept out onto the plain. It resembled the plain I'd crossed with Pie after leaving Klamath Falls, with little islands of solid ground here and there that supported trees whose twisted trunks reminded me of Monterey pines, but whose leaves were ribbony and fluttered in the wind like streamers. Not a sign of life, though I assumed there were fish in the lakes and the waterways that fed into them. It was exhilarating to see, but soon it grew boring, this interminable passage of reeds and lakes and twisted trees. The train appeared to be flying past the same scene repeated over and over. Our initial excitement dissipated, and we sat against the side wall of the car, eating dried fish and jungleberries, talking but not saying much, just "Pass me the fish," and "Want some water?" and "You feelin' okay?" Comforting noises more than conversation.

The sun baked the car at noon, and the heat worked to bring out a lazy heat in us. We made love on our stretched-out sleeping bags, a far different experience from the sport-fucking I'd done on trains in the past, when the rattle of the cars and the noise off the rails drowned out every human sound, causing it to seem that the racket was somehow related to the messy, intemperate character of the act. The winded quiet of our train was like a bed of gentle noise supporting us, enabling sweetness. We fell asleep afterward, and when we woke it had come twilight, and the mountains ahead looked to be considerably closer, their peaks shrouded in a cloudy darkness like battle smoke. We'd be into them by morning, I figured, if the train kept its current pace, and then, maybe, we'd discover if this had been a good idea or merely an ornate form of suicide. The heat faded, the air grew chill, but the car, warmed by its golden blood, kept us relatively cozy. We draped blankets over our shoulders and held hands and watched out the door.

As dusk settled, far out on the plain, what appeared to be a flock of large ungainly birds flapped up from the reeds, their numbers swelling until it covered a considerable expanse of the sky. I noticed the train had picked up speed, and as the flock drew closer, I understood why. Hundreds of black blanketlike objects, their surfaces fattening with wind, their flights unsteady, erratic, making swoops and glides that were more crumpled collapses, but moving inexorably toward us nonetheless. "Oh, shit!" Annie said, and heaved at the door, sliding it shut. I cracked it back open a couple of inches so I could see, and she said, "Are you crazy!" and struggled to push it all the way closed again.

"We need to be able to see what's goin' on," I told her. "Case we have to jump."

"Jump out into this hellhole!" she said. "That ain't gon' happen! Now shut the fuckin' door!"

When I continued to hold the door open, she shouted,

"Goddamn it, Billy! You keep it open, one of 'em's liable to pry at it and get inside with us! That what you want?"

"I'll take the chance. I don't wanna be trapped inside."

"Oh, and I ain't got no say. That it?" She got right up into my face. "You think I come on this ride just so you can boss me around? You better think twice!" She hauled off and punched at me, her fist glancing off my cheekbone, and I fell back a couple of steps, stunned by her ferocity.

"I ain't scared of you!" she said, her shoulders hunched. "I ain't taking no shit off you or anybody!"

Her eyes darted to the side, the muscles in her cheeks were bunched. Seeing how frightened she was acted to muffle my own fear, and I said, "You want it closed, then close it. All I'm sayin' is, if the car starts gettin' tore up, maybe we oughta know what's goin' on so we can make a reasonable decision."

"Reasonable? What the fuck are you talkin' about? If we was reasonable, we'd be back over Yonder and not fixin' to die out here in the middle of nowhere!"

The car gave a heave, a kind of twitching movement, and then gave another, more pronounced heave, and I knew a beardsley had settled on the roof and was tearing at it. An instant later the door was shoved open a foot or so, and another beardsley began squeezing through the gap, like a towel drawn through a wringer, its mottled, bald old man's head pushing in first. Annie shrieked, and I ran to my pack and plucked out my ax handle. When I turned, I saw the beardsley was halfway inside the car, its leathery black sail flapping feebly, the hooks on the underside proving to be talons three and four inches long, a dirty yellow in color. It was such a horrible sight, that parody of an ancient human face, utterly savage with its glittery black eyes and fanged snapping mouth, I froze for a second. Annie was plastered up against the edge of the door, her eyes big, and as the sail flapped at her, the talons whipping past her face, she screamed again.

I didn't have a strategy in mind when I charged the beardsley; I simply reacted to the scream and lunged forward, swinging the ax handle. I took a whack at the head, but the sail got in the way, folding about the ax handle and nearly ripping it from my grasp. I started to take another swing, but the sail gloved me and yanked me toward the creature's head with such force that my feet were lifted off the floor. The thing smelled like a century of rotten socks. Talons ripped my shoulders, my buttocks, and I saw the end of reason in those strange light-stung black eyes . . . and then I saw something else, a recognition that jolted me. But almost instantly it was gone, and I was back fighting for life. I had no way to swing at the beardsley, being almost immobilized by the grip of the sail; but I poked the end of the ax handle at it as it hauled me hard forward again, and by chance, the handle jammed into its mouth. My fear changed to fury, and I pushed the handle deeper until I felt a crunching, the giving way of some internal structure. I rammed the handle in and out, as if rooting out a post hole, trying to punch through to the other side, and suddenly the head sagged, the sail relaxed, and I fell to the floor.

I was fully conscious, but focused in an odd way. I heard Annie's voice distantly, and saw the roof of the car bulging inward, but I was mostly recalling the beardsley's eyes, like caves full of black moonlit water, and the fleeting sense I'd had as I'd been snatched close that it was somehow a man, or maybe that it once had been a man. And if that were so, if I could trust the feeling, how did it fit into all the theories of this place, this world. What determined that some men were punished in this way and others sent over Yonder? Maybe if you died in Yonder you became a beardsley, or maybe that's what happened if you died out on the plain. My suppositions grew wilder and wilder, and somewhere in the midst of it all, I did lose consciousness. But even then I had the idea that I was looking into those eyes, that I was falling into them, joining another flock under some mental sky and becoming a flapping, dirty animal without grace or virtue, sheltering from the sun in the cool shadows of the reeds, and by night rousing myself to take the wind and go hunting for golden blood.

I came to with a start and found Annie sitting beside me. I tried to speak and made a cawing sound—my mouth was dry as dust, and I felt a throbbing pain in my lower back and shoulders. She stared at me with, I thought, a degree of fondness, but the first thing she said was, " 'Pears I was right about the door."

I tried to sit up, and the throbbing intensified.

"I got the bleeding stopped," she said. "But you're pretty tore up. I cleaned you best I could. Used up all my Bactine. But that was a damn dirty thing what sliced you. Could be the wounds are goin' to get infected."

I raised my head—the beardsley was gone, and the door shut tight. "Where are we?" I asked.

"Same as before," she said. " 'Cept the mountains look bigger. The beardsleys flew off somewhere. Guess they drank their fill."

"Help me get up, will ya?"

"You oughta lie down."

"I don't wanna stiffen up," I said. "Gimme a hand."

As I hobbled around the car, I remembered the clutch of the beardsley's sail and thought how lucky I'd been. Annie kept by my side, supporting me. I told her about how I'd felt a human vibe off the beardsley in the moments before I killed it, and what I thought that meant.

"It probably didn't mean nothin'," she said. "You were scared to death. You liable to think almost anything, a time like that."

"Yeah," I said. "But this was real strong."

"So what?" she said. "So it was human, so what? Who cares what it means? You ain't never gon' figure it out. Ain't no point in tryin'. Hell, that's one reason I come with you. I couldn't listen to people's harebrained theories no more. I wanted to go where there's somethin' more constructive to do than sit around and contemplate my goddamn navel."

"You didn't see what I saw," I told her. "You had, you'd be curious, too."

"Fine," she said. "It's a stunnin' development. The beardsleys are human. What's it all fuckin' mean? I won't rest till I get to the bottom of it."

"Jesus, Annie," I said. "I was just speculatin'."

"Well, save it! If we survive this ride, maybe I'll be interested. But right now I got more and better to think about."

I said, "All right."

She peeked at my shoulders and said, "Oh, God! You're bleedin' again. Come on. Sit back down, lemme see what I can do."

In the morning I pushed open the door and had a look round. The mountains loomed above us. Granite flanks rising into fangs of snow and ice that themselves vanished into fuming dark clouds, fans of windblown ice blasted into semipermanent plumes from the scarps. Back in Yonder, the mountains had seemed huge, but viewed up close they were the roots of a world, the bottom of a place boundless and terrible, a border between trouble and emptiness. Their names, if they had names, would be violent hatcheting sounds followed by a blast of wind. They offered no hint of happy promise. A chill bloomed inside me from a recognition of my folly, of having given up on Yonder and put Annie and myself in the way of far worse. But when Annie came to stand beside me, all I said was, "Looks like it's gon' get cold."

She stood gazing up at the mountains and said, "Yeah, looks

like." She went over to the sleeping bags and dug a down jacket out of her pack.

On the outside of the car, next to the door, were several gouges that appeared to be scabbing over with filmy black stuff, the golden congealed blood showing through. I glanced at the mountains again and thought I saw a flash of lightning in the clouds.

"Close the door," Annie said. "We'll be there soon enough. Ain't no use in starin' at it."

I slid the door shut and sat beside her. "It's just mountains," I said.

She gave a sniff of laughter. "Yeah, and Godzilla's just tall."

"I'm sorry. I'm sorry if this turns out wrong. I didn't . . . It felt right to leave."

"I ain't gon' blame you. I coulda stayed." Then after a pause, she said, "I'm glad I didn't stay. I couldn't tolerate Yonder no more."

That surprised me a little, though I'd expected she would come around to admitting it eventually. "We probably don't go way high up in 'em," I said. "Tracks wouldn't get built that high."

"They ain't real tracks and nobody built 'em."

"Well, yeah. There's that." I tried to think of something comforting to say. "'Member the Wizard of Oz? How he had this fearsome voice, but he turned out to be a little fat guy and the voice was fake? The mountains are probably like that."

"Dorothy and the Scarecrow," she said dispiritedly. "That's us, all right." She worked a hand in down among the clothes in her pack and pulled out a deck of cards. "Wanna play some gin?"

So we ate jungleberries to calm our nerves and played cards as the train ascended into the mountains, going over the Wall. We played for a dollar a point, double for gin, and after a while we began to joke and laugh, and for the most part forgot about the wind, which had started howling around the car, and the cold that was gradually seeping inside. Annie kicked my butt for the first hour, but then I had a run of luck and went up several hundred dollars. I dumped the next game to bring us closer to even, and as I shuffled and dealt the cards, I thought of other rides we'd taken both separately and together, beat up and fucked up, drunk and stoned, sick and afraid, and how it seemed all that had been preparation for this ride up into wherever. Maybe it *had* been a form of preparation, maybe the world was so painstaking and intricate in its wisdom that part of its process was to prepare those who failed it for a wild ride into an unknown land. But Annie was right. True or not, it was useless knowledge. It was the kind of thing you did not need to live.

The arguments of doctrine and the study of philosophy, they might or might not have validity, but the only functions they served were either to exercise the mind or, if pursued to excess, to blind you to the bitterness of life and keep you from the more joyful practices necessary to withstand it.

"Hey," said Annie, beaming. "Guess what?"

"What?" I said.

She spread out her hand for me to see. "Gin!"

Midway through the game I had to piss, and when I cracked the door to do so, I found we were rolling slowly through a whitish fog so thick I could barely make out the wheels of the train. Apparently we were down in some sort of declivity, shielded from the wind, because it was howling louder than ever. I thought it must have been breaking off enormous ledges of snow—audible above the howling were explosive noises such as accompany avalanches. Half-frozen, I finished my business and ducked back inside.

"What's it like out there?" Annie asked.

"Like a whole buncha nothin'. Got some serious fog." I sat back down, watched her deal. "We must be down in a pocket."

Done with dealing, Annie studied her cards, glanced at me, and said, "Your turn."

I picked up my hand, made a stab at arranging it. "Fog's not even driftin'. You'd think with all the wind, it'd find some way to blow a little bit down where we are."

"Got any threes?" she asked, and laid down a three.

I started to pick up the card, changed my mind, and drew from the deck. "Maybe it ain't all wind. Maybe it's somethin' else goin' on that sounds like wind."

"C'mon, Billy," she said. "Play a card. Even if it's the last thing I do, I'm gonna beat you silly."

There came a noise, then. A shriek . . . except it didn't come from any throat. It was more an electronic note edged with bursts of static, and it was loud—loud as a police siren suddenly switched on behind you. We dropped the cards, scrambled farther away from the door, and as we did, the shriek sounded again and a brilliant white flash cut a diagonal seam across the door, like someone was outside and swinging a magnesium torch at the car. The heat that came with it had that kind of intensity. The walls of the car rippled, the floor humped beneath us. For a fraction of a second, the seam glowed too brightly to look at, but it faded quickly, and we saw that a rip had been sliced in the door, leaving an aperture about six inches wide and three feet long. I heard distant shrieks, identical to the one I'd initially heard, and thereafter a tremendous explosion that reminded me, in its magnitude, of dynamite charges I'd set when working highway construction the summer after high school. Whatever the car was made of—skin, metal, plastic, a combination of things—its torn substance had been somehow sealed, cauterized, and there was not the slightest seepage of golden blood. We heard more explosions and shrieks, but when after a few minutes nothing else struck the car, we went over to the rip and peered through it. Annie gasped, and I said, "Jesus . . ." Then, both inspired to act at the same time, we slid the door wide open so we could get a better look at where we were bound.

What I saw I need to describe carefully, slowly, though I seemed to see and absorb it all at once. We were barreling along a snow-covered valley, featureless except for boulders that jutted up here and there, a rift that ran straight as a highway between rows of mountains, a diminishing perspective of giants, brothers to the ones ranged along the plain. They were set close together, without any linkage between them, no ridges or shoulders that merged one into another, and this placement made them seem artificial, a landscape that had been created without the restraints of inorganic logic. Cliff faces of black rock broke from their icy slopes. Beneath the smoky clouds that shrouded the peaks, the sky was alive with bright flying things—blazing golden-white, they might have been sparks shaped into the raggedy images of birds. They wheeled and whirled and curvetted everywhere, sounding their electric voices. There were so many, it amazed me that they did not constantly collide. Every now and then a group of several hundred would form into a flock and arrow down to strike the cliff faces, disappearing like a beam of light into a void, and thereafter, following the briefest of intervals, an explosion would occur, producing not fragments of rock and gouts of fire, but violet rays that streamed off toward the end of the valley in the direction we were headed. I had the feeling that I was watching the operation of a vast engine designed to create those rays, but what the rays were fueling—if that's what they were doing—was so far outside the scope of my experience, I had no way to interpret it.

Once when I was drunk in Kalispell, flush from the sale of some copper wire I'd stolen from the freight yard there, I wandered into a souvenir shop and became interested in the mineral samples they sold. What especially caught my eye was a vial of black opals immersed in water, and after studying them for a while, glossy black stones that each contained a micro-universe of many-colored flecks of fire, I bought them for fifteen dollars—I would have stolen them, but the clerk had his eye on me. At the far end of the valley the land gave out into a place similar to those depths embedded in the stones, a blackness that appeared one second to be bulging toward us, and the next appeared to be caving in. Countless opalescent flecks trembled within it, and whenever the violet rays penetrated the blackness, it would flicker as with heat lightning and for an instant I would have a glimpse of something that had been obscured. The glimpses were too brief for me to identify the thing, but I had a sense it was a complicated branching structure, and that it went a long way in . . . Another explosion, and I realized what had happened to the door of our car. As the explosion occurred and a violet ray spat forth, the spark birds closest to it went swerving out of control and tumbled from the sky. Several came swerving low above the train before righting themselves and rejoining the others.

We gazed at the scene until the cold drove us back inside the car, and then we sat huddled together without speaking. I can't say what was in Annie's mind, but I was more awestruck than afraid. The scale of the mountains, the strangeness of all else—it was too grand to breed true fear, too foreign to inspire other than wonder, and too startling to allow the formation of any plan. Hobos, for all their degenerate failings, have an aesthetic. They're scenery junkies, they take pride in traveling through parts of their country few have ever seen, and they memorialize those sights, whether storing them in their memories or creating more tangible mementos, like SLC with his wall of Polaroids. Sitting around campfires or in squats, they'll swap stories about the natural beauty of the world with the enthusiasm of kids trading baseball cards. Now Annie and I had a story to top anybody's, and though we had no one to tell it to, as if by reflex, I polished the details and dressed up the special effects so if I ever did get the chance, I'd be ready to let the story rip. I was kept so busy doing this—and maybe Annie was, too—I didn't notice the train was slowing until we had dropped more than half our speed. We went to the door, cracked it, and peered out. We were still in the valley, the mountains still lifted on either side, the spark birds were still wheeling in the sky. But the opaline blackness that had posed a horizon to the valley was gone. In place of it was a snow-covered forest beneath an overcast sky and, dividing the forest into two distinct sections, a black river that sprung up out of nowhere and flowed between those sections, as straight in its course as that of the valley between the ranked mountains. It was clear the train was going to stop. We got our packs together and bundled up—despite the freakishness of the forest and river, we figured this was our destination, and were relieved to be alive. When the train came to a full stop, we jumped down from the car and set off across the snow, ducking our heads to avoid the wind, which was still blowing fiercely, our feet punching through the frozen crust and sinking calf-deep.

The train had pulled up at the end of the line; the tracks gave out beyond the last mountain, about a mile and a half, I judged, from the edge of the forest. The ground ahead of us was gently rolling, the snow mounded into the shape of ocean swells, and the forest, which looked to be dominated by oaklike trees with dark trunks and heavy iced crowns, had a forbidding aspect, resembling those enchanted and often perilous forests illustrated in the children's books that the old Billy Long Gone had turned to now and then, wanting to read something but unable to do more than sound out a few of the words. When we reached the engine I took the can of spray paint Pie had given me and wrote on the side:

> PIE—
> WE COME TO A FOREST THE
> OTHER SIDE OF THE MOUNTAINS
> IT'S THE END OF THE LINE
> WE'RE WALKING FROM HERE ON
> LUCK TO YOU
> BILLY LONG GONE

"Wanna add somethin'?" I asked Annie.

She studied on it, then took the can and wrote:

> IT'S ALL A TEST
> SO FAR WE'VE PASSED
> ANNIE

"A test, huh?" I took back the can and stowed it.

"I been thinkin' about it," she said. "And that's what I figure it is. It just feels that way."

"Here you always talkin' 'bout you can't stand theories, and now you got one of your own."

"It ain't a theory if you're livin' it," she said. "It's a tool for making decisions. And from now on I'm lookin' at all this like it's a test." She helped me rebuckle the straps of my pack. "Let's go."

We had walked about two-thirds of the distance between the end of the tracks and the forest when one of the mounds of snow on our left shifted and made a low grumbling noise, like something very large waking with mean things on its mind. It was so sudden an interruption to the winded silence, we froze. Almost immediately, another mound shifted and grumbled . . . and then another.

"Run!" said Annie, unnecessarily—I was already in motion, not quite running but moving as fast as I could, plunging ahead, my legs going deep into the snow. There was no wonderment in me now, only fear. We thrashed our way through the snow, the wind cutting into our faces, while all around us were shiftings and ugly animal rumbles. We angled toward the left-hand section of forest, a point not far from where the black river sprang from beneath the earth. The trees seemed to inch nearer, and as I glanced behind me to gauge how close pursuit was—if, indeed, something was in pursuit —I tripped and fell. Annie screamed at me to hurry. As I staggered up, fighting for balance, I saw that several of the mounds had risen to their feet. They were heavy-bodied, slothlike, big as delivery vans, with long silky white hair shaggying their thick legs and backs. The hair fell into their faces, which were mushed-in, startlingly human except for their extremely wide mouths. Their eyes, half-hidden, were bright and violet, the same exact shade as the rays that erupted from the cliff faces. One started toward me, waddling slowly, but gaining momentum, and I plunged forward again, my breath steaming out, heart pumping, trying to will myself ahead and into the shadowed avenues among the trees. Even at top speed, apparently, the slothlike creatures were slow, and I thought we were going to make it. But at the edge of the forest, just as I stumbled almost breathless beneath a low-hanging bough, Annie grabbed my jacket and hauled me to a stop.

"The river!" she said, gasping. "We gotta go for the river!"

"You're outa your mind!" I tried to shake her off, but she clung to me.

"It's a test!" she said. "Like back in Yonder . . . . the mountains looked like the worst option. But we got through 'em. Now the river looks like the worst. That's the way out. I know it!"

The nearest of the sloths was a couple hundred feet away, and about a dozen more were edging up behind him, all grunting as they came, sounding like stalled engines trying to turn over. I started to run again, but Annie kept a hold on me and dragged me down to my knees beside her.

"Godammit, Billy!" She shook me. "They can follow us into the forest! But the river . . . maybe they won't go there!"

The logic of that penetrated my panic. I dragged her up and we went lurching, half-falling, ploughing toward the bank. But on reaching it, I hesitated. The way it ran straight, like a long black sword laid flat across the land, its point invisible beyond the horizon, dividing everything from nothing. The Styx. Charon. Mythic images of death crowded into my brain. The water was flowing up fast from wherever it came. Snow crusts fallen from the bank floated on it. Cold as it looked, I doubted we'd last more than a minute or so. Beneath the surface were glittering points that reminded me of the beardsleys' eyes. The slothlike creatures lumbered near. Their mouths were partially obscured behind fringes of hair, but they were wide enough to swallow us both without stretching. The shine of their violet eyes stained the snow in front of them, as if they were nothing but energy inside, no guts, no bones, just a furnace of violet glare. Their footfalls made no sound. Freeze or get chewed. It was not an easy choice.

"Billy!" Poised on the brink, Annie pleaded with me, but I couldn't take the step. Then her face seemed to shut down, all her caring switched off, as if it, too, had been a light inside her, and she jumped, disappearing from sight with a sodden splash. She did not resurface, and I knew she must be dead, killed by the shock. When I understood that, I didn't much care which way I went to hell.

Behind me, the grunting evolved into a piggish squealing. Two of the animals had begun to fight, batting with their enormous paws, mauling each other, trying to bite with mouths that opened into pink maws the size of loading bays. I watched their incompetent white battle for a second, unconcerned, empty of awe, of fear, of all feeling. I saw the mountains beyond, the sky whirling with sparks, and it seemed I could see all the way back to Yonder, the tree full of hobos, the green river, the jungle, the gorge where Euliss had died. But I could no longer see the world. It was like smoke in my memory, its images dissolving, or already dissolved. Alone and cut off from all I had known, I had little use for life. For no better reason than it was where she had vanished, I jumped into the river after Annie.

What is it we think when we are born? After the shock, the stunning light, the sudden absence of comfort and warmth, the alarming sense of strange hands, the pain of the umbilical knife . . . what apprehension comes to stir the first wordless concern, the first recognition? I think it must somehow resemble the thought I had when I woke in a ferny hollow with Annie and three others: I yearned for the vague particulars of the creature inside whom I had been carried to that place, whose knowledge of the place was in me, albeit cloudily realized as yet. A creature whose skin might be a river or the interior of a black boxcar, and whose geography incorporated Yonder and places of even deeper strangeness. A vast, fabulous being whose nature was a mystery to me, but for the fact that it engulfed the world like a cloud, a heretofore unobserved atmosphere, nourishing the earth as an oyster nourishes a pearl, and extracting whomever it might need for its purposes. A great identity whose presence had been unknown to everyone; though certain saints and madmen may have mistaken it—or recognized it—for God, and those who dwelled long years in the solitudes might on occasion have sensed its sly, ineffable movements beyond the sky (old Euliss Brooks might have been one such). A cosmic monstrosity who had strained the stuff of my mind through its own substance, purifying and educating me toward an end I could not yet perceive. Before I opened my eyes and learned that Annie was there, I realized I was as different from the Billy Long Gone who had jumped into the river as he had been from the man who had climbed drunkenly aboard a black train in Klamath Falls. Smarter, calmer, more aware. I had no clear memory of where I'd been, but I understood that Annie had been right—this was a test, a winnowing, a process designed to recruit a force of considerable measure from among those who lived on the edges of things, from loners and outcasts, and develop them into . . . what? That I was not sure of. Pioneers, explorers, soldiers? Something on that order, I believed. But I did know for certain that those who failed the test became part of it, transformed into beardsleys and worse, and those who survived went on to take part in some enterprise, and I knew this because the creature who brought me to the hollow had imprinted that knowledge and more on my brain.

The hollow was spanned by the crown of a tree with a thick grayish white trunk and milky green leaves. The sky was overcast, and the air cool like summer air at altitude, carrying an undertone of warmth. I felt no weakness, no fatigue—in fact, I felt strong in all my flesh, as if newly created. I looked at the others. Apart from Annie, who was just beginning to stir, there were two men and a woman. One man, lying on his back, eyes closed, was dark, lean, bearded. Dressed in a fatigue jacket, blue pin-striped trousers that must have belonged to an old suit and were tucked into boots. Next to his outflung left hand were a small backpack and an automatic rifle. The other two were asleep in an embrace. Brown-skinned; tiny; wearing rags. Mexican, I thought, judging by the man's Aztec features. I picked myself up, went over to the bearded man, and examined his rifle. Words in the Cyrillic alphabet were incised on the housing. To be on the safe side, I pocketed the clip.

I checked on Annie—she was still asleep—and then scrambled up the slope of the hollow. When I reached the top I saw a city sprawling across the hills below, surrounded by forest on every side. On the edges of the city were new shacks and cabins carpentered from raw unpainted boards and logs. The buildings farther away were older, weathered, but not many were larger than the buildings on the outskirts, and they were only two- and three-stories tall. It was like a frontier town with dirt streets, but much bigger than any I'd ever heard of. A shanty metropolis. People were moving along the streets, and I made out animals pulling carts . . . whether oxen or horses or something else, I could not say. But the city was not the dominant feature of the view. Rising from its center, vanishing into the depths of an overcast sky, was an opaque tube that must have been a hundred yards in diameter, and along it were passing charges of violet light. It was half-obscured in mist—perhaps the mist was some sort of exhaust or discharge—and this caused it to appear not quite real, only partially materialized from its actual setting. I knew, in the same way I had known all else, that the violet lights were men and women going off on journeys even more unimaginable than the one I had taken, traveling through the branching structure I had glimpsed back in the valley (the tube was merely a small visible section of the structure); and that the city was the place to which they returned once they accomplished their tasks. Knowing this did not alarm or perturb me, but the implication it bred—that we were still inside the thing that had snatched us from our old lives—was depressing. Understanding had become important to me, and I had believed I would eventually come to an understanding that would satisfy my need for it. Now it was clear that I would always be in the midst of something too big to understand, be it God or cosmic animal or a circumstance that my mind rendered into a comprehensible simplicity . . . like God or a cosmic animal. I would never be able to climb up top of any situation and say, "Oh, yeah! I got it!" For all I knew, we could be dead.

I heard a noise, saw Annie scaling the slope toward me. She gave me a hug and took in the view. "Well," she said. "I was right."

"I never doubted it."

She put an arm about my waist and squeezed. "You lie."

We stood looking across our new home, calm as house buyers checking out a property, and I was actually starting to think where it was we might settle—would it be better on the edge or downtown close to the tube?—when our three companions came to join us atop the rise. The Mexican couple glanced at Annie and me timidly. They stared impassively at the vista; the woman crossed herself. I was surprised that she retained the traditions of her faith after having traveled so far and learned so much. Maybe it was a reflex.

"English?" the bearded man asked, and Annie said, "American."

"I am Azerbaijani." He squinted at me and scowled. "You take my bullets?"

I admitted that I had.

"Very smart." He smiled, a clever, charming smile accompanied by an amused nod. "But rifle is broken. Bullets no good."

He gazed out at the city with its central strangeness of opacity and violet fire. I wanted to ask if he had ridden a black train to some Azerbaijani halfway house and how he had traveled the rest of the way, and what he thought was going on; but none of it was pressing, so I joined him in silent observance. Considering the five of us, the variance of our origins, I thought I was beginning to have a grasp of the mutability of the unknowable, of the complexity and contrariness of the creature god machine or universal dynamic that had snatched us up. And this led me to recognize that the knowable, even the most familiar articles of your life, could be turned on their sides, shifted, examined in new light, and seen in relation to every other thing, and thus were possessed of a universality that made them, ultimately, unknowable. Annie would have scoffed at this, deemed all my speculation impractical woolgathering; but when I looked at the tube I reckoned it might be exactly the kind of thinking we would need wherever we were going.

The sun, or something like a sun, was trying to break through the clouds, shedding a nickel-colored glare. The Mexican woman peered at each of us, nodded toward the city, and said, "*Nos vamos?*" Annie said, "Yeah, let's go check this out." But the Azerbaijani man sighed and made a comment that in its simplicity and precision of vocal gesture seemed both to reprise my thoughts and to invest them with the pathos common to all those disoriented by the test of life.

"These places," he said musingly, then gave a slight, dry laugh as if dismissive of the concern that had inspired him to speak. "I don't know these places."

Jailbait

IRON HORSE WAS, IN MADCAT'S ESTIMATION, A true thoroughbred among fortified wines and every bit the equal of Night Train. The packaging, which depicted a brazen fire-breathing stallion in full gallop, contrived a perfect visual analog to the charge it had made through his bloodstream. Two pints had trampled his anxieties, flattened out his migraine, and enabled him to view with contentment the sorry particulars of his place in the world: a bridge on the edge of the Spokane freight yard, an abutment spangled with graffiti rising to a vault of discolored concrete that roofed the cardboard pallet where he rested with legs asprawl, head propped against his pack, a wiry, weathered man of thirty whose ragged beard and gaunt features presented an image of Old Testament fortitude. His left eye was bloodshot, the skin around it discolored from a beating, and a less recent scar ridged the cheekbone beneath it. Now and then he would sit up straight and warm his hands at a fire gone to embers, gazing blearily about, while the rush of traffic overhead fell around him like the surging of invisible tides.

Beyond the bridge lay a muddy, rutted ground dappled with snowy patches and slicks of dead grass. Railroad junk strewn everywhere. Rusting wheels, dismantled brake shoes, and objects less definable nested in the weeds along the tracks. A waste bordered by stacks of railroad ties and dark gatherings of boxcars, all sketched in glints and gleams by the shining of a high-flying half moon, so the place looked to have acquired the cozy, comprehensible geography of a village and an air of romantic isolation it did not possess by day. Somewhere off in the yard two cars coupled with a steely clash. The forlorn voice of a train, as questioning as a whale's song, sounded the greater distance, and with its fading, a shadow slipped from behind a stack of ties and darted toward the bridge, resolving into a slight, pale girl with unnaturally red hair and dressed in baggy clothing. She stopped about forty feet away and peered at Madcat, trying —he supposed—to make certain he was harmless. Then an engine unit came chugging out onto the section of track behind her, like a huge yellow-and-black mechanical dog sniffing at her heels, and she scooted forward again. She stood hugging herself just beneath the lee of the bridge. Dyed scarlet dreadlocks hung down over a sharp, thin-boned face. Skin so white as to seem nearly translucent. Pretty . . . but the sort of witchy Appalachian prettiness that never lasts much past twenty. Her sweatshirt and carpenter's pants rubbed gray with grime. Still hugging herself, she edged a few steps closer, and once the noise of the engine had abated, she asked, "Kin you he'p me, mister?"

"I kinda doubt it," Madcat said.

The girl's head twitched as if the flatness of his response had touched a nerve.

"I got no money to spare, that's what you're asking," he said.

She glanced nervously back toward the yard and when she spoke, her voice had a catch in it. "Kin I set here a minute? Kin you jus' lemme set here and not bother me?"

That irritated him. "Set wherever the fuck you want."

She hesitated, then dropped to her knees beside the fire and stretched her hands out over it—as if conjured by the gesture, a tiny flame sheeted from the bed of embers, brightening the glow on her palms. Madcat caught a whiff of creosote and thought she must have been standing close to the ties for quite some time to pick up that smell.

He cracked the cap of his third pint, had a swallow, and considered the girl. Her eyes were shut tight, squeezing out tears. Yet for all her apparent helplessness, the tense, forward-thrusting attitude of her neck and the thick scarlet twists of hair caging her white face gave her an uncanny look. He imagined she was casting an evil spell and the tears were the result of concentrated effort. She made a fretful noise in her throat, drew a breath that pulled the sweatshirt taut across her breasts.

"Want some wine?" he asked, holding out the bottle.

Her eyes snapped open and went toward it, the way a snake will quicken on spotting a mouse. She shook her head, sat back on her haunches. "There's somethin' I should tell you 'bout," she said.

"Oh, that's okay," he said. "I got enough troubles, I don't need to be taking yours on."

"Naw, I 'spect you gon' wanna hear this." She hooked three of the scarlet snakes with her fingers, dragged them back from her face. "Me and Carter . . . this boy I met. We was smoking a joint—" she gestured toward the yard "—over in there somewheres. I had to go pee and I was comin' back . . . I's 'bout to crawl 'tween two cars to get to where Carter was settin'. And that's when I seen this shadow rise up behind him. This man." She made the words "this man" into a question. "He had a club or somethin'," she went on. "He didn't say a word, he just stood there a second like he's thinkin' things over, then he hit Carter in the head. Carter went flat on his face and he hit him again. He kept on hittin' him even though there wasn't no point to it. I could tell Carter was dead." She stared into the embers. "I don't reckon he seen me. I sure didn't see him—he had his back turned the whole time I's watching." She looked pleadingly at Madcat. "I didn't know where to turn. I mus' been an hour wanderin' round out there 'fore I run into you."

The scattery way she talked out the story made him think she didn't believe it—or maybe putting it into words had rendered it unbelievable. It rang true enough to him. "You better get on home," he told her. He struggled to his feet, back-pocketed the pint.

"Home?" She gave a shaky-sounding laugh. "I'm a long way from home, mister."

He shouldered his pack, settled the straps. She came to one knee, alarmed, and asked what he was doing. "Long as I can catch out on a freight train," he said, "cops ain't gon' find me hanging 'round no fucking crime scene." He headed out into the yard, trying to shake off his buzz, and she scrambled after him. "But you didn't do nothin'!" she said. "You got nothin' to worry 'bout!"

"You think that, then you don't know shit about cops." He picked up his pace.

"Kin I come?"

She was standing with knees together, hands clasped, head tipped to one side, the pose of a little girl left behind by older kids. Framed by the cathedral-like sweep of the bridge, she looked—with her strange punky hair—the picture of innocence freshly corrupted. He had the sense she knew the impression she was making.

"I never rode the trains before. Carter, he was gonna teach me . . ." She brought her clasped hands up to her chest. "I won't be no burden, I swear. If you want I kin be with you. Y'know?" Meeting his gaze, she seemed to back away from commitment. "For a while, anyways," she said. "If you want."

He wasn't sure he was interested in what she was offering—he'd been a long while without, almost three years, and most of his memories of women had to do with the trouble they landed you in and not the sweetness they brought.

"All right," he said, after giving the notion a couple of turns. "But don't go thinking you can count on me. All that's happening here is we're taking a train ride together. I'm nobody you want to be counting on."

Often after one of his spells, and sometimes during them, Madcat would dream about trains—not the Union Pacific freights he was used to, but supernatural beings, mile-long metal snakes coiling around the switchbacks through a snow-peaked mountain range that went on forever, the only alive things in all that noble wilderness. Usually the dreams had a certain sinister quality, and this one started out no differently, with an old-fashioned black steel locomotive powered by an enormous human heart instead of a furnace, but then it changed in character, a variance of degree alone, because there was always an element of the sinister involved, and he thought that Grace—this, the girl told him, was her name, and she was from Ohio and had been living in squats, hanging out, surviving, but she was sick of the life and was heading to California to hook up with a rich uncle . . . He thought that Grace, then, must be responsible for this change. The locomotive, which was twice normal size, spat scraps of fire from its stack and howled like the ghost of a giant, but as they sped deeper into the night the howling gentled down into music, thunderous at first but growing increasingly easy on the ears, and streams of pink and aqua light mixed with the ebony smoke pluming from the stack, and the scraps of fire turned into glowing ankhs and crescents and all manner of Cabalistic sign, a torrent of bright arcana flowing back along the body of the train, enveloping it, so that the car where he and Grace were sheltering was transformed into a radiant space with the ambiance of a weird night club —like a retro neon sign come to life—where dancing silhouettes followed the elaborate suggestions of artfully dissonant strings and saxophones that sprayed clusters of mathematical symbols from their bells, and he and Grace were dancing too, gliding off to join the other featureless, faceless couples, buoyed up among syncopated martini glasses, tuxedo-wearing stick figures, old dream-blue drifts of jazz and smoke-ring Saturns . . .

He woke to find that the freight had pulled off onto a siding. His face was stiff from exposure and a back tooth was throbbing. Winter light shafted through the cracked door of the boxcar, shining upon frozen particles of dust so they looked like silver atoms. He and Grace had wound up spoon-style in the sleeping bag, and his erection was prodding her behind. He tried to shift away, but only succeeded in rubbing up against her.

"I cain't sleep with you poking me," she said muzzily. He unzipped his side of the sleeping bag and she protested: "I didn't mean for you to get up!"

"I gotta piss," he told her.

The cold floors stung his feet; he went on tiptoes to the door and peeked out to see if anyone was checking the cars. Fresh snow blanketed an expanse of rolling hills, framing rectangles of golden winter wheat. An ugly smear of egg-yolk yellow had leaked up from the eastern horizon; elsewhere the gunmetal blue of the sky had gone pale at the edges. The train was a local, stopping at every shit-hole, and Madcat figured they were still a ways from Missoula. He let fly and his urine brought up steam from the gravel.

"I hafta pee, too," Grace said.

He dug a roll of toilet paper from his pack, tossed it to her, and went back to the door. A few seconds later she jittered up beside him, doing a hopping dance to fight the chill. In the sunlight her red hair was even more startling in contrast to her pallor, reminding him of a *National Geographic* photo he'd seen of African dancers with white clay masks, their hair dreaded up, caked with dried mud. She gave him a nudge, trying to move him aside, and said, "Lemme out."

"You gotta do it over in the corner," he said. "You go outside, brakeman or someone's liable to see you."

She squinched up her face but otherwise made no complaint.

Up ahead, about a quarter-mile from the tracks, lay a tiny reservation town. Trailers, shanties, rusted pickups. One trailer pitched at a derelict angle, slipped partway off its blocks. Clouds with pewter edges and blue-gray weather heavy in their bellies were pushing in low from the north.

The sound of Grace's water tightened his neck.

It took him several minutes to stop shivering after he got back into the sleeping bag. He drew up his knees and turned onto his side, facing the wall. Grace propped herself on an elbow, leaned over him. A rope-end of her hair trailed stiff and coarse across his jaw, and he scratched where it tickled.

"You like my hair?" she asked.

"It's all right. Doesn't feel much like hair."

She pretended to dust his nose with the bristly end and giggled. "I'm the same color down below," she said. "Know that?"

"Guess I do now."

She was silent a few ticks, then: "Why you so paranoid 'bout the cops? I mean I know what you said about 'em's true, but you was in an awful hurry last night."

He started to tell her to fuck off, but decided she was entitled. "My wife had an affair with a cop. I came home one afternoon, and they were going at it in my bed. I jumped on top of 'em and beat the shit out of him. I knew they're bound to file charges, and with both him and my wife testifying, no way I wasn't gon' do some time."

"So you took off runnin', huh?"

"Went down to the yard and caught out on my first freight. I was just too sick to deal with all that lawyer crap. I'd been getting these headaches, blackouts and shit, for a couple years, and I couldn't work. Doctor thought maybe it was job-related. Environmental. But wasn't no way to prove it." He eased onto his back and rolled his shoulders, working out a stiffness. "No money coming in, the wife gets unhappy, she goes to humping Dudley Do-right." He made an embittered noise. "That's my story. The Making of a Hobo. Reckon I can sell it to the movies?"

She didn't appear to notice that he had made a joke. "You still sick?" she asked.

"I get spells now and then."

With a shattering rush, a train stormed past on the adjoining track, and speech became impossible. The shadow of its passage caused the light to flicker like the beam from an old projector. Grace settled beside him.

"You know," she said after the last car had gone by, "I bet my uncle could he'p you with them charges, I's to ask him. Man must have a dozen lawyers workin' for him. Maybe you should come on down to LA with me and see what's what."

" 'Round Tucson's where I like to winter," he said.

She snuggled closer and the warmth of her body seeped into him; soon his erection returned.

"'Pears you gon' have trouble sleepin'." Her fingers traipsed across his thigh. "Want me to take care of that for you?"

He felt oddly shy and looked away from her. "Yeah. Sure . . . whatever."

"Now that's what a girl wants to hear." She removed her hand and mimicked his delivery. "'Sure . . .whatever.' Hey, I can go on back to sleep if you're not interested. But if you are, it'd be nice to know I's bein' 'preciated."

"I appreciate it," he said.

"That's a little better, but still . . ." She cupped his face in her hands. "C'mon, tell me somethin'. Say."

Her irises were a deep, dark blue, the same hard color that held at the top of a midafternoon winter sky, edged with bits of topaz and gold like the geometric scraps you find inside a kaleidoscope. "I want . . . " he said, and then, a little fazed by her closeness, lost track of things.

"Well, there you go," she said. "I almos' believed that one."

The freight rolled eastward. Grace's arms and legs were tomboyish, lean, the architecture of her ribs plain to see, but her breasts were heavy, the skin soft as crepe and so pale that the veins showed through. Blue highways on the map of a snowy country. She braced on his chest with one hand, straddled his hips and fitted her blood-colored bush to him. The tightness of her took his breath. "I know you like that," she said, straightening above him. "I can tell jus' how much you like it." She reached back and pulled the sleeping bag cover up behind her as if it were a vampire's cape, shrouded herself in it so that only wintry blue eyes and scarlet hair were visible of the terrible white creature she was pretending to be. Then with a fang-bearing hiss, she sank down atop him, enclosing them in a rattling darkness that lasted all the way to Missoula.

That night they showered up and ate at a mission in Missoula, then skipped out on the preaching and spent much of the next day obtaining emergency food stamps, which they sold for fifty cents on the dollar to a mom-and-pop grocery. They bought supplies, mostly wine, and Grace found herself some clean clothes and a used knapsack at the Goodwill. During rush hour she worked the sign, stood at a busy intersection holding a piece of cardboard upon which she'd written *Please Help Me Get Home*, and took in close to a hundred dollars—that gave them more than two hundred to travel on, even after spending twenty-six on a motel with In-Room Triple XXX Adult Videos.

"Why cain't we do like we done in Spokane?" she asked the following morning as they labored up a hill west of town, moving through a stand of old-growth pine, heading for a section of track that climbed a steep grade. "Whyn't we jus' go in the freight yard and find us a car?"

"Spokane's a pussy yard," Madcat said. "Any damn fool can catch out of Spokane. In Missoula the bulls'll bust your head open, then run you in for trespassing."

It was good traveling weather, cold and clear, gusting a bit. Patches of sunstruck needles like complicated golden ideograms trembled on the forest floor, and every so often the dark green pinetops would lift in a flow of wind and sway all to one side with the ponderous slowness of dancing bears. When they reached the tracks Madcat had Grace tie off the cuffs of her jeans with an extra pair of shoelaces so they wouldn't catch on anything. "We gon' be looking for a grain car," he said. "Got a little porch on the front end where two can ride. Now when it comes it won't be going real fast, but it's going faster than it looks, so don't try and jump on it. You gotta respect the steel. You go throwing yourself at it, you liable to wind up underneath the train. What you do is, you grab hold of the hand rails and let your feet drag along in the gravel till you feel under control. Then you can haul yourself up."

The side of the hill had been cut away, leaving a cliff of pinkish stone looming above the tracks. They sat with their backs against it, gazing out over the forested slope. Madcat sipped from a jug of Iron Horse and Grace fired up a hand-rolled, then exhaled a glowing cloud of smoke that boiled furiously for an instant in the strong sun.

"Where's this train taking us?" she asked.

"Klamath Falls, Oregon. Got a big switchyard there. Won't be hard finding something heading for Tucson."

"I cain't understand why you won't at leas' consider going to California," she said querulously.

"'Cause I'm going to Tucson. Cops there don't give a damn 'bout a few tramps drinking their wine and smoking their dope. And that's how I like things."

"Yeah, but if you's to come to California, my uncle might could he'p you with your legal problems."

"Your uncle got himself a cement pond?" he asked.

She looked at him askance. "What you talkin' 'bout?"

"I want to know if he's got a cement pond, 'cause the only hillbilly bitch I know's got a rich uncle in LA's named Ellie Mae Clampett." He had another swallow of wine and felt a sudden ebullient rush, as if that swallow had enabled him to commune with the group consciousness of drunkards, to tap into their reservoir of well-being. "I guess it's possible a homeless redneck female talks like you, all ungrammatical and shit, could have herself a doting uncle with a big bank account. And I suppose this uncle could have such a fine liberal sensibility, he'd be inclined to extend himself on behalf of the unemployable alcoholic who's fucking his niece. But I gotta tell you, it seems like a long shot."

She flipped away her cigarette and stared at him meanly. "You don't believe me 'bout my uncle? You sayin' I'm lyin'?"

"I'm saying I intend to winter in Tucson. You want to go with me . . . great. If not . . . " His expansive gesture indicated a world of possibility beyond the horizon.

"I jus' don't understand you." Grace lowered her head so that her face was shrouded in dreadlocks—to Madcat's eye they resembled the alluring tendrils of an anemone; he imagined tiny fish trapped among them, dissolving in a haze of scarlet toxicity. "Ever' time I say anything you disagree with," she went on, "you treat me so cold. I don't know what I do to deserve it."

"Cold? I'll tell you what's cold! Cold's a woman watches her boyfriend get his brains bashed in, then a few hours later she's jammin' with some tramp."

"I tol' you Carter wasn't my boyfriend! I didn't know him more'n couple hours, and all we did was smoke a joint, talk a little. It ain't like we had a relationship."

"What about us? We got a relationship? I get my brains bashed in, how long you figure it'll be 'fore you feel up to having consensual sex?"

She looked out toward the cobalt line at the ends of the earth. "I do what I hafta to survive. I'm no differnt 'n you." She gave him a sideways glance. "Yeah, I think we could have us a relationship. Leas' we got some 'sperience of one another and it ain't killed us yet. You might discover you like me a lot, you stop tryin' so hard to pretend you don't."

The burst of energy that had fueled Madcat's contentiousness faded and he sat nursing his pint, listening to the pour of the wind, trying to hear in it the chunky rhythms of an approaching train.

"What's your real name?" Grace asked.

"Jimmy."

"Jimmy what?"

"Jimmy That's All You Fucking Need To Know. Okay?"

"Okay! Don't get your panties in a bunch!" Then, after a pause: "How'd you get your train name? You make it up yourself?"

His response was to affect a moronic laugh.

"I should get myself a name, I guess, I'm gon' be ridin'." She made a show of thought, tapping her chin with a forefinger and squinting, clicking her teeth with her tongue. "I cain't come up with nothin' sounds right. Maybe you should gimme a name."

A powerful lethargy overcame him and the patch of gravel between his feet seemed to acquire topographical significance, as if it were the surface of an alien planet seen from space—a flat of cracked granite lorded over by a single dusty weed so vast, the minuscule creatures who dwelled in its shadow would perceive it as a pathway to the divine and send forth pilgrims who would die in the process of ascension.

"Jimmy!" Grace spoke with such urgency, it penetrated his fog.

"What?" he said, sitting up straight. "What is it?"

She was tying off her dreads with an elastic band, gathering them into a Medusoid sheaf behind her head, studying him without expression. The shadow cast by her raised elbows was like a mask of gray wings that came down onto her cheeks, and he knew death was in her, that whether sent or by herself commanded, she had come to gather him. He tried not to believe it, though the truth was clear and undeniable, like a letter graven on her brow. He felt a satin pillow beneath his head and saw his eyes reflected by a mirror inside a coffin lid.

"Nothin'," she said, giving a dry, satisfied-sounding laugh, as if some critical judgment had been borne out. "Never mind."

Near nightfall of the next day, they jumped off the train outside the Klamath Falls yard and pushed their way through thickets of leafless bushes with candy wrappers, condoms, cigarette cellophane, and toilet tissue stuck to their twigs, so profuse they might have been some sort of unnatural floral productions. A line of dusky orange marked the horizon, dividing darkness from the dark land, and a west wind was blowing with a feverish rhythm, gentle gusts alternating with featherings, then long oceanic swells carrying streaks of unseasonable warmth. As he slogged over the mucky ground, Madcat, coming off an afternoon drunk, broke a light sweat.

Two hobos were jungled up in a clearing near the edge of the yard, hunched beside a crackling fire, drinking malt liquor. There was Horizontal Tom, a scrawny old man whose ravaged face peered out from snarls of iron-gray beard and hair like a mad hermit spying from behind a shrub, and F-Trooper, a lanky man in his forties with straight black hair hanging to his shoulders, an adobe complexion, and a chiseled, long-jawed face that might have been handsome if not for its rattled expression. Wearing chinos and a tattered AIM T-shirt. When he caught sight of Madcat he got to his feet, picked up two forty-ounces, and went to do his drinking elsewhere. "Fuckin' Indian motherfucker," Tom said with some fondness. "He just can't abide too much company, but otherwise he ain't so bad."

"Son of a bitch can't abide me is what it is," Madcat said. "I ain't never said shit to him, couple times we met, but he always acts like I been kicking his dog."

"Hell, he acts like that with ever'body. Took him five, six years to warm up to me." Tom bunched his sleeping bag up around his head, fashioning it into a cowl. "Could be he's just shy."

"Yeah, uh-huh." Madcat sank to his knees by the fire, Grace beside him. "You and him riding together?"

"Nah. I come out on a hotshot from Dilworth couple days ago. Found him campin' here. He's waitin' for somethin' headin' down to Roseville. Me, I'm—"

"Roseville's in California, ain't it?" asked Grace.

"If you wanna call Sacramento California." Tom had a pull from his bottle, and some of the brew dribbled out the side of his mouth, beading up in the tangles of hair, glittering in the firelight—his face shadowed dramatically by the cowl, he might have been an old philosopher-king with jewels woven in his beard. "I'm headin' for Mexico," he went on. "Copper Canyon. Ever been down that way?"

Grace allowed that she had not.

"Big as the Grand Canyon and never been exploited, 'cause they ain't no roads to it. Only way to get there's by hoppin' a freight." Tom grinned, showing eight or nine teeth banded with brown and yellow stains like the stratifications on canyon walls; he pitched his voice low. "They got organ-pipe cactus been there since the conquistadors. Ol' great-granddaddy iguanas seven foot long." He reached across the fire and poked Grace's knee. "You oughta ride down with me and see it. It's amazin'! Like campin' out in the middle of a goddamn hallucination!"

"I figure we're gonna lay up in Tucson a while," Madcat said. "But we might make it down there eventually."

Grace excused herself, saying she was going to find a place to camp, and went off into the bushes, dragging Madcat's pack. Tom tracked her backside out of sight. "That's a reg'lar little ditch witch you got yourself there. How'd you two hook up?"

Madcat told him. "I don't know if I believe her 'bout the boy getting killed," he said. "She exaggerates some."

"These days there's always somebody goin' 'round killin' out here." Tom shook his head somberly. "It's the drugs. They ruint the rest of society, now they ruinin' things for the hobo." He spat into the fire, and a tongue of orange flame flickered back at him. "How old you figger she is?"

"Seventeen, eighteen . . . I don't know."

"Eighteen might be pushin' it," Tom said, after due consideration. "She looks like jailbait to me. These crusty punk girls, seventeen's 'bout when they get to feelin' wore down, they start wantin' to find themselves a man they can depend on. Sixteen . . . all they want for you is to take 'em somewhere on a train. But seventeen's when they go home . . . if they gotta home. Or they latch onto an older man." He leaned toward Madcat, intending—it appeared—to give him a friendly nudge, but found he couldn't reach that far, wobbled, and nearly fell into the fire. "You be a fool not to let her latch onto you," he said on regaining his balance. "She's 'bout the best-lookin' thing I seen out here. You was to take her to Britt, to the hobo convention, she'd be like Raquel fuckin' Welch compared to them hairy hogs show up there."

Tom seemed to lose the thread of what he was saying, stared off toward the yard. Glowing pinpricks were visible through the dead twigs—sentry lights at the edge of the yard—and a distant clamor could be heard, a windy mingling of bells and whistles and metallic thuds.

"'Member Jabberjaw? That ol' girl I was ridin' with a few years back?" Tom asked. Madcat said, Yeah, he sure did, and then Tom said, "Jesus Lord, I have slept with some scary-lookin' women."

He began talking about old girlfriends, then about hobo marriages he'd witnessed, ceremonies variously uniting Misty Rose, Diamond Dan, Dogman Jerry—and Madcat took to imagining a ceremony involving himself and Grace. They were standing on a flatcar that was being pulled by four white locomotives running abreast on four silver tracks, on wheels that were bleeding, and they were passing beneath a sky bigger than a Montana sky ruled by two black suns and a high-flying half moon, a thousand light years of dark wintry blue and a filigree of clouds like feathers, fishbones, lace. Grace had on a T-shirt and jeans and a circlet with a veil behind to cover her hair—a Maid Marian cap—and her face was chalky, dead calm, but the scarlet dreadlocks were seething beneath the veil, and the ring in the palm of her hand was alive, a golden worm eternally swallowing itself . . .

He coughed, gave his head a shake, and found he was staring

through a maze of leafless twigs at one of the sentry lights. Drunk, oblivious to all else, Tom was still chattering away. Rock-and-roll music was playing somewhere nearby, and Madcat could hear Grace's laughter coming from the same general direction. He heaved up to a knee and peered toward the yard.

"Oh, yeah," said Tom behind him. "You might want to check on that. That's been goin' on a while now."

Madcat staggered through the bushes, slapping branches aside, and soon emerged onto a black plain that smelled of cinders, and stretched to the limits of his vision. Near at hand the plain was criss-crossed by tracks, with here and there a stray boxcar or two; several hundred yards farther in lay an area of furious activity, blazing spotlights sweeping across shadowy trains, engine units shuttling back and forth, brightly colored repair carts trundling about; and in the farthest reaches was a tumultuous area of white glare and roiling smoke from which the darkly articulated shapes of mechanical cranes surfaced now and again, moving with the jerky imprecision of science fiction insects.

Grace was dancing along a section of outlying track, shaking her ass, lifting her hair up behind her head, and F-Trooper was stumbling after her, holding a forty ouncer and a portable radio. He got right on her butt and thrust awkwardly with his hips, almost dry-humping her, and when she danced away, he said, "Whoa! Awright! Unh-yeah!" and then with a sodden laugh hurried to catch up. Watching them, Madcat felt anger, but anger partially occluded by the vagueness and unease that sometimes preceded a migraine.

"Hi, Jimmy!" Grace caught sight of him and waved cheerfully. "You through talkin' to your friend?"

F-Trooper weaved to the side and stood with his legs spread, gazing stupidly at him.

Madcat walked over to Grace, the friated soil crunching beneath his boots; he grabbed her arm and said, "Come on."

She pushed at his chest, tried to break free, and said, "Fuck you! Jus' who the fuck you think you are?" She tried another break, flung herself away, whipped her head about. Her dreadlocks whacked him in the face, and he let go, reeled backward. Then he heard her yell, "Jimmy! Watch out!"

F-Trooper had dropped the radio and was charging at him, preparing to swing his bottle. Madcat stepped inside the swing, seized two handfuls of the man's hair, and headbutted him, simultaneously bringing up a knee. The Indian blocked the knee, but Madcat butted him again and that dropped him. He kicked the man hard in the ribs, the stomach, then in the tailbone as he crawled away. F-Trooper flopped onto his back. "Aw shit . . . Jesus!" he said. Blood slickered his forehead.

"Fuck you trying to do?" Madcat turned to Grace, who had taken refuge off along the tracks and was managing to look at once horrified and delighted. "You want to ride to California with this fuckwit? That what this is about?"

"Naw . . . un-uh!" She hustled over to him, took his face in her hands, and whispered, "I think he's the one, Jimmy. He's the one killed Carter."

"Bullshit!" He shoved her away, took a few unsteady steps back toward the camp. The pressure in his head was building, the migraine about to spike.

"I swear!" she said, coming up beside him, still keeping her voice down. "That's why I's bein' so nice to him. I was tryin' to find out stuff. He told me he was in Spokane same night we was."

Madcat made an effort to focus. Her dreadlocks appeared to be quivering, and her eyes gave back hot glints of a sentry light. "You told me you never saw the guy's face," he said, and planted a fist against his brow to push back the bad feeling.

"Un-uh! I said he had his back to me. I could see some of his face, I jus' couldn't see it all. But I'm pretty sure now he's the one. What you think we should do?" When he did not answer, she leaned into him, pressing the softness of her breast against his arm. "You don't have to worry 'bout me goin' nowhere, Jimmy. I really care 'bout you. Ain't I proved it?"

She was always working two propositions, he realized, prepared to switch off whenever one or the other proved untenable. Maybe she believed in both—who could say? Whatever, there would always be these tests, one of which he would eventually fail . . . though, he also realized, thinking back to her shout of warning, it wasn't clear that she'd leave him even then. It was like they were married already, working behind that fabulous sacramental inertia.

"You havin' one of your spells? You are, ain'tcha?" She linked arms with him. "C'mon back to camp. I fixed it up real nice. Made us a lean-to and ever'thing. You get some wine in you, you'll feel better. You kin sleep and I'll keep watch 'case that asshole tries anything." She cast a wicked glance back at F-Trooper. "Not that I think he will. 'Pears you busted his little red wagon all to hell."

As she led him toward camp, from behind came a sound of breaking glass. F-Trooper had thrown his bottle at them, missing by a wide mark. He was sitting slumped forward, his legs spread, like a big bloody baby; the busted radio fizzed and clicked by his side. The skin of his forehead had split open, painting his face a glistening red, and he was so badly lumped up above the eyes, it put Madcat in mind of atomic mutants in movie monster magazines. Witness gave him no pleasure. It was not a good thing to be reminded that a man who had hit rock bottom could always find a deeper place to fall.

"Fuckin' . . ." F-Trooper's voice thickened and he had to spit. "Goddamn fuckin' malt liquor!" The weak force of his glare seemed to be carried by a breath of wind that stirred black motes up from the tracks. "I'd been drinkin' whiskey," he said in a piteous tone, "I'd a kicked your ass!"

It must have been a random noise that woke Madcat, an operation of pure chance, unless God or something whispered in his ear, saying, "Man, you better get your scrawny butt up or else you be sleepin' a long time," and why would any deity worth a shit bother with the likes of him. . . ? Yet he couldn't quite reject the notion that some lame-ass train god, an old smoke-colored slob with a dead cigar stuck in his mouth, wearing a patched funeral suit and a top hat with a sprung lid, still had some bitter use for him and had flicked a grungy black finger to send a night bird screeching overhead, sounding the alarm. Whatever the cause, when the roof of the lean-to was ripped away, his eyes were open and he was sufficiently alert to roll off to the side and then went bellycrawling into the bushes.

Grace was screaming, F-Trooper was roaring curses, and all Madcat could see was dark on dark until he got turned around and spotted the sentry lights. He scrambled up, a broken twig scoring his cheek, and made for them, bursting out of the thickets and sprinting some fifty feet out into the yard. There he stopped and called back: "Grace! You all right?"

F-Trooper stepped out from the thickets, more shadow than man, carrying an ax handle at the ready. He was holding his ribs, and his movements were cautious, rickety; but Madcat had no desire to go against that ax handle. He was still half-drunk, uncertain of his own physical capacities, and though the rough ground tore at his bare feet, he set off running, aiming for the center of the yard. If it hadn't been for Grace, he might have tried to lose F-Trooper among the trains and then headed for the mission in Roseville where he could hustle up a new pair of boots. But as he ran, glancing back at his pursuer, he noticed that the Indian was losing energy with every step, and Madcat soon discovered that he was able to maintain a secure distance by merely jogging. F-Trooper staggered, flailed, stumbled, occasionally fell, and finally began to run in a low crouch, huffing and grunting, arms nearly dragging on the ground, like a man undergoing a transformation into some more primitive form. Madcat slowed his pace further.

They had entered that portion of the yard where earlier there had been tremendous activity. It was quiet now, and dark. No spotlights, no handcars, no repair carts. The train the crews had been putting together was ready to go. Madcat led F-Trooper down a narrow avenue between two long strings of cars. Container cars, flatcars, 48s, grain cars, boxcars. With their great painted monograms— SFR, UP, XTRA, and such—dully agleam in the thick night, and looming so high that only a strip of moonless sky was visible overhead, they had the gravity of sleeping beasts, creatures whose hearts beat once a millennium, their caught breaths hardened into cold iron. Madcat went to walking sideways, watching F-Trooper reel against the cars like a drunk trying to negotiate a narrow hallway. Spittle hung from his jaw, and his eyes were like bullseyes, the pupils completely ringed by white. When it was clear that he had reached the point of exhaustion, his gait reduced to an enfeebled limp, Madcat turned to confront him. F-Trooper's face displayed a stuporous resolve—he continued his approach without giving the slightest sign of anger or fear, faltering only when his legs betrayed him. Drawing near, he swung the ax handle, but the swing was weak and off balance. Madcat had little difficulty catching his wrist and wresting the club free. He butt-ended the man to the jaw and F-Trooper crumpled without a sound, collapsing onto his side, one arm outflung behind him, half-resting beneath the porch of a grain car.

The violence adrenalized Madcat, washed away the residue of drunkenness. He felt amazingly clear-headed. Clearer than he had felt in a long while. Under ordinary circumstances, muddled with wine, he would have tossed the ax handle aside and set off to find Grace; but now he realized there was an important decision to be made. If he were to walk away, leaving things as they stood, he would likely have cause to regret it. F-Trooper, in his judgment, was too far gone to reason with and obviously not the sort to forgive and forget. The last thing Madcat wanted was to be happily sloshed in a jungle somewhere and have the Indian sneak up behind him. It was bound to happen sooner or later. He and F-Trooper traveled the same roads. This was something that had to be done. Purely a matter of self-defense.

He grabbed F-Trooper by the shirt, pulled him from beneath the car, straddled the body. He tightened his grip on the ax handle. The Indian's head lolled to the side and he let out a guttering noise, half gargle, half snore. With his bruises and lumps and cuts, fresh blood stringing from the corner of his mouth, a brewery stink rising from his flesh, he was a thoroughly pitiable item. Madcat was terrified by the step he was about to take, in the sight of a judgmental God. A preemptive strike was called for, a threat to his security had to be neutralized. Though the logic of nations would carry no weight in a court of law, such was the basis of ethical action on the rails, where men carried their paltry kingdoms in their packs. He had no choice. But as he lifted the ax handle high, he was struck by a sudden recognition, less than a recollection yet sharper than an instance of *déjà vu*, and he seemed to remember, almost to see himself standing in this same position with a half moon flying overhead and at his feet a teenage boy sitting cross-legged in a patch of weeds. It was only a partial glimpse, as if a flashbulb had popped inside his skull, illuminating a confusion of shadows too complicated to allow certain identification; but the shock of it sent him staggering back. He lost his footing on the uneven ground and sat down hard, scraping his hands on the gravel. The idea that he might have committed a senseless murder during a blackout, and that muscle memory or a faulty circuit in his brain had rewired him to the moment . . . it roused no great revulsion in him, no shiver of moral dismay. But the knowledge that he must have sunk to some troglodyte level where conscience no longer even registered, where unrepentant viciousness was part of the human circuitry, that knocked away the last flimsy props of his self-respect.

F-Trooper groaned. Soon he would regain consciousness, but Madcat was too addled, too disheartened to act. All his clarity was evaporating. Then a compromise occurred to him. He crawled over to F-Trooper, wrangled off his belt, lashed his hands, and secured the free end to the grain car's porch, immobilizing him. This done, Madcat fell back and lay gazing up at the sky. Whatever moon ruled, it was hidden behind cloud cover baked to a dusty orange by the reflected glare of Klamath Falls. He tried to deny what he'd imagined he had seen, telling himself that, with his headaches and the drinking, he was liable to see anything—hell, his brain was on the fritz most of the time, buzzing and clicking like F-Trooper's busted radio. Even now he was having trouble stringing thoughts together. So many feelings and facts and memories were churning inside him, his head was like a room in which too many conversations were going on for him to make sense of any one, and a golden hole was opening in his vision, the way a hole gets burned into a piece of paper by bright sunlight directed through a magnifying glass, and he heard a hosanna shout so vast it might have been braided together out of every shout of joy and tribulation ever uttered, and he realized that all the sound and light causing his confusion was coming from a train.

This was no old-fashioned steam-powered locomotive, but a Streamliner, one of those trains named Zephyr or Coronado, an emblem of 1950s Futurism with double-decker lounge cars and a Silver Streak-style engine, only this particular engine was gold with a green windshield, so the effect was of a great sleek golden beast wearing emerald shades. It was speeding straight at him, radiating the sort of holy sunrays that artists usually depict emanating from Buddhas and Krishnas and Christs, and it was taking up every inch of space between the strings of cars. He braced for the impact, squeezing his eyes shut. Yet somehow it missed him and roared on past—he caught sight of Grace's dreadlocks whipping out the engineer's window. He thought he was safe once the last car had gone by, but the train's speed was such that the draft sucked him up like a scrap of paper and he went bouncing along behind it, banging down onto the rails and flipping up, skipping over the ties. It hurt like hellfire. His legs snapped, bones splintered and poked out his flesh. But he had no regrets. He'd known Grace was trouble from the get-go, and maybe that was why he had hooked up with her, maybe he'd been looking for that kind of trouble—things had not been going well, and the best he could have hoped for was a few more bad years, years of drunkenness and headaches and blackouts, before he was knifed or shot or died of life's own poison. This way, at least, he'd gotten to feel some things he'd forgotten how to feel, because though Grace was, at heart, no-account, she knew how to make it sweet, this farewell ride, this little going away party with the lowlife angel of death.

The train receded down a golden tunnel, dragging with it the bloody fragments of his imaginary corpse, and the headache that followed left Madcat curled up in pain beside the rails, unmindful of everything around him. The pain was so intense, it formed a barrier between the moment and all that had gone before, and when at last it abated, it took him a while to notice that the grain car to which he had lashed F-Trooper was missing—the entire string of cars was missing – and longer yet to comprehend that the grain car had been part of the train put together earlier in the evening, and now, with F-Trooper attached, was gone off on its run. He stared at the patch of gravel where the Indian had fallen, numbed by the terrible character of the death. Moving awkwardly, stiffly, he got to his feet. He found he was still holding the ax handle and let it fall. It wasn't his fault, he told himself. It was the world. This world of mystical steel and cheap wine and lonesome fuck-ups in which even an act of mercy, and that's what it had been, no matter how fuzzily motivated it seemed at the time . . . even an act of mercy could result in blood. But of course it was his fault. He couldn't escape what he had done, nor could he escape what he might have done in Spokane. The boneyard reality of it all bred a weakness in his limbs; he thought he could feel some feathery, insubstantial thing fluttering behind his brow. He started trudging back toward the thickets, following the remaining string of cars, stopping now and then to lean against them.

Parked about fifty feet from the end of the string was a police cruiser, startlingly white and defined against the bleak topography of black dirt and curving tracks. The sight brought Madcat up short. His instinct was to run, but he had no energy left. The longer he stood there, the more alluring became the prospect of ceding authority over his life to the competency of jailers and the consolation of lawyers, to a controlled environment with hot meals and daytime TV and card games, even if in the end it led to the injection. The police car fascinated him. It was empty and appeared to be talking to itself in angry squawks, as if it had developed the power of human speech and was cursing the desolation amidst which it had been abandoned. When Grace called to him, before he spotted her coming across the yard, he half-believed the car had succeeded in mimicking her voice.

"You crazy?" she said. "The cops is ever'where! They 'rested your friend, but I hid our stuff out so far from the fire, they never seen me." She tugged at his arm. "C'mon! We gotta get goin'!"

"Think maybe it was me killed your boyfriend?" he asked.

Dumfounded, she peered at him through the raggedy curtain of her dreads. "What?"

"Back in Spokane. Was it me?" He turned his back to her, held his arm up as if brandishing a club. "This look like what you saw?"

Incredulity showed in her face. "Naw, it was that Indian fella . . . I'm almos' positive."

"It coulda been me," he said. "Coulda been me in one of my blackouts."

"It was the Indian." She shot him a dubious look. "F-Troop or whatever. Why you goin' on this way?"

What if it were true? he wondered. What if he'd rid the world of a murderer? What were the odds of that—of anything—being true? He couldn't be sure that Grace was being straight with him about the dead boy. Could he have convicted himself of a murder that had never been committed? He would have liked to force the truth out of her, but he knew her well enough to understand that once she swore something had happened, she would never forswear it, however improbable the facts made it appear. The things that were truest for her were the lies she relied on, and if one or another accidentally turned out to be true, it would still come out a lie in her head.

"C'mon, Jimmy! Le's go!" She pulled harder on his arm, yet her expression gave scant sign of emotion. Her face seemed in its frail angularity the face of a wicked androgynous fairy peeking from among scarlet rushes, not quite hiding a knowing smile. Perhaps he misread her, perhaps that almost imperceptible curvature of the lips merely reflected a degree of strain. But that, in the end, was why he let her drag him away—the intimation that her secret self was peeking out from behind the clownish surface she usually presented to the world, and that she wanted something other than protection on a long train ride, that she signified an ending more intricate than death, and had some sly and delightful, albeit not yet formulated, transmortal purpose for which she now intended to save him.

Unless you were a runaway child and fell prey to one of the many pedophiles who frequented the area, the Salt Lake City freight yard could be an agreeable place for someone wanting a free train ride. The bulls had little interest in tramps, and the crews were a generally friendly bunch, an attitude that manifested in their habit of leaving a few boxcars open on every train that went out. Madcat and Grace had located such a car and were sitting with their backs against a wall, looking out the door, which was cracked so wide it might have been a picture window offering a view of a fireball sun declining behind snow peaks.

"What we gon' do for money in Tucson?" Grace asked out of the blue.

"The usual. Maybe pick up some day work here'n there."

Grace fingered the edge of the sleeping bag. "I waited tables in this fancy cocktail bar one time—made me some serious money. If I had a job like that, maybe we could get us a place. Not for forever, y'know. Jus' for a coupla months. Be nice to have our own place for a coupla months, wouldn't it?"

"Might," he said. "Long as we stay away from rent hassles. I had enough of that shit."

"You don't need to say nothin' 'bout that. I'm with you there."
She tucked in her chin and inspected the front of her new sweatshirt, smoothed out the ironed-on decal of a fluffy white kitten.
"Y'know, I think we're startin' to learn 'bout each other. We're gettin' to where we can start workin' stuff out."

A kid with a shaved head, wearing an army jacket and jeans, was
angling toward the car, cutting across a weedy patch. Madcat kept
an eye on him.

"It's like with now," Grace said. "I'm okay with goin' to Tucson,
'cause I wanna make you happy. But that don't mean I'm givin' up
on takin' you to visit my uncle. I figger it'll come time when you'll
wanna do that for me."

The kid took a stand some twenty-five feet away and stared at
Grace. His neck was heavily tattooed, his facial jewelry picked up
glints of the dying sun. Grace didn't appear to notice him. Her
mime-pale face wore a distracted expression as she contemplated
some fictive future. Madcat vibed a warning at the kid, cautioning
him to get his Road-Warrior-looking ass the hell and gone.

"I think you gon' be surprised," said Grace. "Two people get
together, neither one of 'em knows what's gon' happen at first. But
after 'while—" she groped at the air, like an artist trying to describe
a half-imagined shape "—you can sorta feel how it's gon' be."

You don't know what's in me, Madcat beamed at the kid. Hell,
I don't know myself. But you don't want to find out.

A thin ridge of cloud like the coast of a rugged country hovered
above the peaks, dark gray hills and cliffs of cloud washed to blood-
red underneath.

"Ain't like I kin see it or nothin'," said Grace. "If I could—" she
gave a snort of laughter "—we wouldn't never have no troubles. I'd
jus' draw us a map straight on to wherever it is we're bound."

The kid spun on his heels and set out east along the tracks, head
down, hands thrust in his jacket pockets, as if disappointed in life.

"And where's that?" Madcat asked. "Where it is you figure we're
bound? Besides Tucson, I'm talking."

"I don't know." Grace shrugged, the blithe gesture of a child
responding to a question that didn't concern her; then she cut her
eyes toward him and for an instant she became visible in the way
she had back in Klamath Falls—a clever spirit with unguessable
motives. "There's one thing I do know. You think you-'n'-me's jus'
about me givin' you sugar, and you takin' care of me. But I'm gon'
be doin' my share of takin' care of you from here out."

The cloudy coast was breaking up into islands and floating

castles, and the sky was separating into bands of color—a broad swath of scarlet behind the peaks edged by a narrow strip of paler red, bordered in turn by a still narrower strip of orange, then the thinnest stripe of peach, and above all that a reach of aquamarine, a color with the sort of mineral purity that you can see behind the clouds in museum paintings of old Italian angels.

Entranced by this evolving masterpiece, Grace said, "You always pokin' fun at things I say. You like to tell yourself the only reason you ever ask me anything is so's you kin get a laugh. But you hear what I'm sayin'. I kin tell. People get close, they bound to change one another. They make each other weaker or stronger. That's why the preacher don't say for better or worse or in case things stay the same." She rested her chin on her drawn-up knees, still gazing at the sky which was developing a cinematic symmetry, balconies of gaudily colored cloud arrayed against a backdrop dominated by great blades of sanguine light—a majestic sight that seemed to bear slight relation to the shriveled-up ball of fire that had produced it. "You'n me, we gon' be strong!" Grace went on. "We gon' shake things up. Know why? 'Cause I ain't lettin' you be weak. You gon' be my strength, but I'm gon' be your heart."

She continued talking, but the conviction ebbed from her words and her speech grew increasingly fragmented, disconnected. Soon she stopped altogether, and Madcat, who had been lulled and persuaded by her voice, felt that he had been hurled from a place in the sky to a cold boxcar floor. The heavy silence of the yard made him think everything was listening, watching, and uncomfortable in the sight of God, he shifted about, trying to restore his psychic equilibrium. Grace settled back against the wall and let out a sigh that seemed to express the recollection of some sad certainty. Then she pointed to the sky and said, "I reckon it mus' be California that way."

Three thousand copies of this book have been printed by the Maple-Vail Book Manufacturing Group, Binghamton, NY, for Golden Gryphon Press, Urbana, IL. The typeset is Elante with Swing display, printed on 55# Sebago. Typesetting by The Composing Room, Inc., Kimberly, WI.